MURDER, SHE WROTE

BY THE TIME
YOU READ THIS
I'LL BE GONE

MURDER, SHE WROTE

AN ORIGINAL NOVEL BY

STEPHANIE
KUEHN

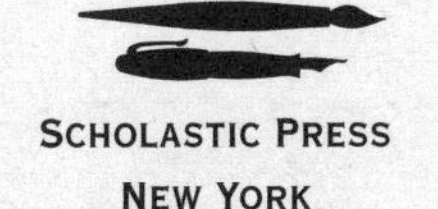

SCHOLASTIC PRESS
NEW YORK

Library of Congress Cataloguing-in-Publication Data available.

ISBN 978-1-338-76455-0

10 9 8 7 6 5 4 3 2 1 22 23 24 25 26

Printed in the U.S.A. 40

First printing 2022

Book design by Keirsten Geise

For those with good motives.

HOME ABOUT NEWS ARCHIVE

TRUEMAINE.COM

Home Page for the State of Maine . . . and Murder . . .

"Death, Disrupted"

I was twelve when I first heard about the Lambert murder. It was the day the Sussman triplets became b'nei mitzvahs. The celebratory afterparty was held at the Ocean View Country Club in my hometown of Cabot Cove, Maine, where it was—and still is—the biggest social event I'd ever attended. Wrapped in a lace shawl and a yellow silk dress my mother had once owned, I can remember huddling outside behind the banquet hall with a dozen or so other kids. There, a scruffy waiter on a smoke break regaled us with the story of a dead girl.

Thirty years or so earlier, he told us, his uncle had worked for the club's groundskeeping crew. This uncle arrived early one morning to repair a faulty sprinkler valve only to discover a dead body on the golf course. A gruesome sight—the victim was a teenage girl, and she'd been strangled, left for dead, her limbs twisted beneath her like a felled deer resting atop the lush emerald green grass.

"Who was she?" my friend Jackson had asked, because that was the most important part of the story to him. This girl, this long-ago dead girl, she was someone, a real person, and to Jackson, her humanity would always come before the lurid details surrounding her death.

Chrissy Lambert, the waiter replied. That was the girl's name. She was seventeen, a rare beauty, and not only was she someone, she turned out to be *somebody*—the daughter of the late George Mitchell Lambert III,

Cabot Cove's very wealthy and much beloved mayor at the time. This fact, above all else, ensured that the town's full resources were poured into finding her killer.

Only no one ever has.

So now this is where I come in, and perhaps you do, too. To this day, Chrissy's case still haunts me, and as a resident of Cabot Cove, my goal is to finally track down her killer. To be sure, in the years since her death, far better sleuths than me have attempted to do the same. They've chased down every lead, followed every clue, only to come up empty.

But thanks to both modern technology and the power of the TrueMaine family, I believe we can achieve what they couldn't by pooling our efforts and working toward a common goal. Only we'll do it methodically—this is New England, after all—and true disruption requires discipline. Think proof of work, not propaganda.

In upcoming columns, I'll highlight what's currently known about the crime, who the early suspects were, and how Cabot Cove reacted in the aftermath. Meanwhile, hit me up in the comments if you have any information about Chrissy Lambert's death or the circumstances surrounding it. We're all safer when we work together.

Until then, be watchful, my friends! Killers walk among us. Statistically, at least one of them knows your name . . .

Yours truly,

—the Downeast Girl

Sign up for our newsletter!

1

"HEY," I SAY WHEN JACKSON finally answers the phone. Like me, he's stayed in tonight, opting out of attending our school's homecoming game and related festivities. There're good reasons for this, but we're definitely in the minority with our choice. A recent social media check featured post after post of our highly identifiable classmates engaging in acts of pregame debauchery before packing the bleachers to cheer on the hometown Cabot Cove Devils in their annual matchup with the South Harbor Seals.

On the other end of the line, Jackson Glanville yawns. Loudly. Clearly, I've woken him. Or at least that's what he wants me to think.

"Don't play coy, Bea," he says. "This is the fifth time you've called. I assume there's some sort of emergency unfolding."

"I wouldn't have to call so many times if you actually answered your phone. Or responded to my texts."

"Texting's not secure. We've talked about this."

"So now you think the feds are reading your messages?"

"When did I ever mention the feds?" He lowers his voice. "They could, though, you know. Us Glanvilles aren't to be trusted."

I laugh because this is what Jackson wants me to do. To pretend I don't hear the current of fear and paranoia running through his voice. To pretend I don't know how much he's suffering.

"Don't worry," he says brusquely. "I'm not going all conspiracy theory on you. The only people I'm worried might be spying on me are of the homegrown variety."

"Well, I'm relieved to hear it."

"So why *are* you calling?"

I bend to double knot the laces of my Caribou boots. "Maybe I just like the sound of your dulcet voice."

"How flattering," he says. "Hey, I read your latest column, by the way. The one you just posted."

So he *wasn't* asleep when I called. I knew it. "What'd you think?"

"Did you have to mention me by name?"

"I said good things!"

"Yeah, well, my dad might not see it that way. He'll probably ground me for being in the presence of nicotine over three years ago. You know how he is. 'If you were truly committed to God's path in your heart, then your body would follow . . .'"

"I'm sorry," I say quickly. "I won't do it again."

"Nah. Don't worry about it." Jackson forces a shot of bravado into his voice. "I'm just being my usual dramatic self."

"You're not dramatic."

"How's that whole thing going?" he asks. "Writing for that true crime site?"

"Well, I'm averaging about three readers a post, but also

they're not paying me. Kind of hard to tell who's coming out on top there."

"They're really having you lean into the cryptocurrency lingo, huh? The disrupting Downeast Girl. Plus all that 'proof of work' stuff?"

I laugh. "My theory is that both owners are heavily invested in Bitcoin. But it's not such a bad metaphor, is it? Cyber detectives as the modern-day crypto miners. It's all decentralized work being generated by anonymous internet users. I think it fits."

"Did you just say *modern-day crypto miners*?"

My cheeks warm. "You know what I mean."

Jackson pauses, and the thing is, I've known him so long that I can picture him perfectly. Right now, he's up in his room with the door locked, and I'm positive he's shirtless. Given the option, Jackson's always shirtless, which is beyond annoying, although he looks great and he knows it. He's probably pacing, too, long legs carrying him back and forth in front of the wide bay window that spans the length of his bedroom. Plus, I'd bet anything Jackson's staring out at the ocean, watching the dark waves churn beneath him as he ponders—not for the first time—what it would feel like to sink. To lose himself in those watery depths.

And look, morbid as that is, I *get* it. Despite our friendship—or maybe because of it—it's been years since I've personally stepped foot inside the Glanvilles' sprawling showcase waterfront home. But suffice to say there's a reason for that.

It's also the reason I'm calling.

"Jax," I say softly.

"It's an analogy, by the way. Not a metaphor."

"What?"

"The crypto mining thing."

"Oh." A quick glance at the clock tells me it's past time to get to the point. "So do you think you can meet up tonight? Are you able to get out?"

"Where?" he asks. "When?"

"At the Hollow. Thirty minutes."

Jax groans. "I *hate* that place."

"I know you do."

"Those Broadmoor kids make me want to puke."

I sigh. Jackson rarely has anything nice to say about the local boarding school or its two hundred or so snobby inhabitants. "Well, tonight those Broadmoor kids are going to be your alibi."

"Hold on." His voice tightens. "Do you mean—"

"Yes," I say as my heart starts to pound. My palms start to sweat. Is this really happening?

Are we really going to do this?

"I'll be there," he tells me, then hangs up.

I grab my stuff and go.

×××

Outside in the darkness, frigid air nips my cheeks, stings my eyes. I gird myself by zipping my fleece coat and cinching the hood as tight as it will go as I make my way into town on foot. There's a saying in Maine that the farther north you go, the more resilient Mother Nature makes you. This is meant to explain our hardiness, our rugged core of self-reliance, but if you ask me, "natural selection" works just as well.

It's a twenty-minute walk under good conditions. But it's Friday night and football means people are out and ready to let loose. Not just high schoolers, either. Cars, SUVs, even a few semis whiz dangerously close as I follow the narrow shoulder of the coastal highway. I've seen enough roadkill out here over the years that I don't dare risk crossing to the ocean side. Not after nightfall. But trust me, that's where the better view is. Even by moonlight you can see over the cliffs and down to the craggy beaches, swirling mist, and pounding surf below.

More cars race by, some honking, and a few passengers even take the time to roll down their windows to yell, wave, pound the paint, and make other—less generous—gestures at me. I can't understand what they're saying, and it seems early still for the game to have ended. But the general spirit of their efforts tells me that somehow, some way, our side's emerged victorious.

This isn't a total surprise. Cabot Cove High's football team is notoriously terrible—as in, our school should cut their funding and spend the money on stuff that actually has a positive impact on students, like, you know, teacher salaries and the girls' volleyball team. But our rival school, South Harbor, has had a serious run of bad luck this year. Okay, luck's an understatement, because what really happened is that two of their players were killed in a car accident back in July. A third came down with Lyme disease during preseason, and now their star quarterback abruptly withdrew from their school just *last weekend*. Rumor has it he's got a drug problem and failed a test, but I've also heard it was an overdose. Regardless, it's not exactly a miracle that we beat them this year, and I'm not sure that it's even worth celebrating. Feels a little like cheering for a win after the other team's bus breaks down.

"Go *Devillllls*!" I duck right as a beer can flung from the open window of a pickup comes flying at me. Missing my head by inches, the can ricochets off the asphalt, and I watch as it spins, sparks, then skids into the grass. Whirling around, I'm ready to confront whoever's responsible, but the truck's long gone. Screeching tires leave the air charred and smoke-filled as the pickup's red taillights swerve across the center line then back again before fading into the fog.

Heart pounding, fists clenched tight, I continue my march onward while allowing my mind to indulge in a series of gruesome revenge fantasies that I'll never have the courage to act on. It's times like these when I lament not having my license yet. There're still six whole *months* until I can take the test, which is practically an eternity in high school years. Everyone in my grade is driving already, and this includes Bobby Miller, who's riding a D average these days and spends most of his time doing donuts in the marina parking lot. But that's what I get for having the audacity to skip third grade. No good deed goes unpunished, and in the eyes of the law—not to mention my dad's insurance policy—raw intelligence holds no bearing on personal liberty.

Well, there are greater injustices in this world, which is why I'm meeting up with Jackson tonight. He and I have been friends since grade school. It's been more off than on over the last couple of years—until recently, that is. But Jackson's troubles run deep. They always have, though you wouldn't know it to look at him. At school, he represents that most perfect of clichés: He's seemingly got it all. From his reluctant rock star good looks to a starting spot on our school's all-state basketball team. Not to mention he's, like, a genius. His academic ranking's top of the class, and for the past two years he's been a part of this statewide accelerated science program you have to be invited to apply for. He's already got his college sights set on the Ivy League. Maybe MIT or Caltech, if they're lucky.

But if appearances can be deceiving, then Jackson Glanville could make a liar out of just about anyone. His bright-eyed ambition and endless accomplishments don't stem from drive or passion or even God-given talent. No, his striving is the very twisted consequence of having been raised by a pair of sadists who equate fear with morality and obedience with virtue. I used to think this was a religious thing—Jackson's dad is an ex-military officer turned Episcopalian deacon. But there's nothing spiritual about the way the Glanvilles treat their son—like he's fundamentally rotten to the core and their job is to prevent him from spoiling the rest of the world. I've had to talk Jackson off more than a few ledges over the course of our friendship. Some of them literal. Anyway, he's recently been offered a lifeline—one I've helped to arrange—and my goal tonight is to ensure he takes it.

My muscles tense as I approach downtown Cabot Cove. There's so much *life* out tonight. Sparkling confetti from the earlier parade litters the street; red, white, and blue ribbons snap from light poles; and the whole atmosphere swirls with postgame revelry. It's infectious, even catching up with the tourists spilling out of the overpriced seafood restaurants and brew pubs running along Main Street. Live music blaring from the speakers at Neptune's Palace adds to the chaos, plus my phone won't stop buzzing. I pull it from my pocket and see messages from Evie, Dane, Roo, everyone—they're all heading to Rock's Head Beach for a bonfire. *Where are you?* they ask. *Game got called at halftime. Too many injured Seals. Arf arf arf. Get out here already.*

Well, this explains the early celebration, and the invitations are tempting. I'm a sworn introvert, but even I can get behind an evening on the beach with people I like, one that ends with salt in my hair and sand in my shoes. They're good people, too, the kind who don't mind my awkwardness or my inability to get out of my head. Only none of them are Jackson, and I won't let myself be distracted. I can't. Not tonight. So rather than respond, I switch off notifications, slide in my earbuds, and hit play on the podcast I've been listening to. It's different than what I usually go for. Rather than a deep-dive true crime story, this is an audio drama—a fictional one. It's about a murder that takes place on a ship and it's told Rashomon-style with its cast of characters rotating to share their version of events as the listener tries to solve the crime along with them.

Like I said, fiction isn't my usual preference, but this came recommended by a family member whose taste I trust without question. "It's the writing," she told me, gripping my arm with an eagerness that felt electric. "You have to listen all the way through. Then listen to it again to figure out how they pulled it off. It's genius. These writers, whoever they are, know precisely what matters in a mystery."

"What's that?" I asked, because I've always assumed that what matters most in a mystery is whether or not the case gets solved.

But she disagreed, emphatically. "The solution's the least important part."

"Really?"

"Yes, really." Her blue eyes twinkled as she pressed her lips into the most inscrutable of smiles. "You see, I've always believed mysteries aren't about uncovering what's hidden so much as shining a light on what you've always known, deep down, to be true."

Yeah, well, I'm not sure what I think about that. As someone who dreams of becoming an investigative reporter someday, true crime doesn't interest me because it somehow manages to represent the totality of human experience or whatever. Honestly, I kind of like when it does the opposite by refusing to hand out easy answers or offer pat platitudes about tragedy. I also like when it asks us to confront the most slippery parts of ourselves. The parts that so rarely end up in fiction because they're the hardest to own and easiest to look away from.

This is the tone I aspire to with my cold case column for TrueMaine, which is the newly launched brainchild of two Portland tech bros aiming to fill the gap between Nextdoor and Netflix. Regardless, this fictional podcast is just what I need at the moment—something that can hold my attention without demanding more. And it's not like good writing and storytelling don't have their place in crime reporting. Story's always what draws me in, and if nothing else, this show's been darkly entertaining so far.

Murder or no murder, there are a lot of ways to be trapped in this world, and I know I'd hate to be stuck on a ship with a group of strangers. Even more, I'd hate having my survival hinge on learning how to depend on said strangers.

What could be worse than that?

2

DOWNTOWN SURRENDERS TO THE GRITTIER side of Cabot Cove. Peeling paint and cracked sidewalks begin to pop up as I move away from the water. I pass darkened storefronts containing such small-town gems as Hello, World! Computer and Mobile Phone Repair, Perfectly Pawsh Pet Salon, Body on Maine Fitness, Gerald's Rare Books and Vegan Donut Emporium, an unnamed store selling vacuum cleaner parts "by appointment only," and finally, the *Central Cove Gazette*, our local paper.

Beneath my boots, the road rises, leading into the foothills. There's not much to see out this way—a few pockets of fifties-era residential homes and one newer development of "luxury estates" that's in the process of being built. This northwest section is also where the Cove's burgeoning biotech sector resides. And by burgeoning, I mean two medium-size environmental engineering companies whose presence and partnership with the state have done a lot to recruit and retain young talent and create jobs for our residents.

This happens to include my dad. As a microbiologist who studied at Michigan, he never would've come back to Maine otherwise, although I can't imagine him living anywhere else. He grew up here, had one of those rugged and charmed childhoods filled with hiking, camping, rock climbing, and ice fishing. Maine wisdom and stubborn practicality run through his veins, guide his life choices.

Some people find these qualities cold, I guess. After Mom died, there was worry from her side of the family that Dad wouldn't know how to support me emotionally. There's valid concern in this; Mom was Black and Mexican, and Maine's about as white as it gets. Combined with my personal fixation on death and disaster—along with the fact that I couldn't sleep for months after the funeral—it'd be easy to conclude this environment might not be the healthiest for me. But Cabot Cove's where my mother chose to live, where she chose to raise me, and I can't leave that. I can't leave *her*.

I don't know that I'll ever be able to.

Cutting across the corporate parking lot of Dad's company, Bio-Mar, I pick up the wooded trail leading to the Hollow. It starts with a series of zigzagging stone steps cut into the hillside that expose you to shear winds and dizzying heights. Technically, you could make it all the way up to Broadmoor Academy this way, although there are easier, less dangerous routes. But the century-old boarding school's presence is undeniable. It looms from above, stern and foreboding, nestled atop the highest peak in this stretch of winding coastal mountains.

Luckily, I'm not headed that far. The Hollow is the agreed-on meeting spot between locals and boarders, although the truth is that we don't tend to mix all that often. Personally, I don't pay much attention to Broadmoor. Having grown up in its shadow, the school's always felt like the perfect metaphor for how rich parents try and shelter their children by locking them away in a literal castle and calling it an education.

I pause as I reach the top of the staircase. As predicted, the Hollow stands empty. Not a lot's here anyway—just a narrow clearing in the woods with a view of the ocean that isn't regularly patrolled by cops. But what makes the Hollow distinctive is the enormous treehouse that generations of teens have added to over the years. Spanning the clearing and built across no less than six separate trees, the structure consists of a creaky fire hazard maze of ladders and rooms and crawlspaces and secrets. Staring up at the rickety floorboards, I hear a faint soft scratching coming from somewhere inside. Mice or roof rats, I bet. The place is probably infested.

With a shudder, I pull out my phone and check the time. The walk took me twenty-five minutes. No sign of Jackson or the red North Face jacket he's always wearing, so I return to the stone steps, where I sit and wait. It's a gorgeous night for it. The waiting, that is. The moon's waxing, harvest bold and hunter bright, and the reflection off the water makes the stars and sky feel endless.

Still, there's no Jackson.

I check the time again and suck in a whiff of air. *Damn it.* We're definitely going to be late now, and I don't get it. I thought he wanted this. That's what he said at least.

That's what it seemed like.

My phone buzzes in my hand. Relief washes over me, until I look and see the text's not from Jackson. It's from my longtime shrink, Dr. Wingate.

You two still coming? We start in five.

Sorry. Can't find J. I'm trying.

Everything okay?

I hope so. Thanks for checking in.

There's no response after this, so I try calling Jackson, and I text him again, too, despite his warnings about surveillance. No answer.

The back of my neck starts to tingle.

This is bad, something inside me whispers.

Really bad.

I work to tamp my rising dread, telling myself to stay calm, to breathe, to stay grounded, but it's too late. The panic's already loose, coursing through my veins like a viper to poison my brain with a flood of worst-case scenarios. Most center around disappointing someone I admire, which is one of my deepest fears. Also, it's actually happening. For months, I've been begging Dr. Wingate to let me bring Jackson to his Friday-night therapy group without parental consent. There was no other way to get him there, I'd argued. His parents were too strict, too controlling. Too insidiously cruel. And tonight, finally, Dr. Wingate had agreed.

But I'm also gripped by a different fear. One that's darker

and almost too terrible to name. It's a fear I live with daily, and it's the reason I'm still in therapy, still on my meds, even after so many years. But as long as I have people in my life who I'd die for, who I'd do anything for, it'll always be here, will always ensure my beating heart rides raw and open on my sleeve.

It's the fear of losing someone I love.

3

NINE FIFTEEN. AT THIS POINT, all hope is lost. Jackson's not coming, and if he does, it's too late. The therapy group's started, which means there's no way we can show up at Dr. Wingate's. Not without being disruptive. Not without being rude.

Shame warms my cheeks as I stand, brush dirt from the seat of my pants, and peer down the staircase into darkness. My brain pinwheels in search of an answer. Maybe Jackson's parents came home unexpectedly and blocked him from leaving. They would if they could. If they had any hint of his betrayal. But that's not likely. They're off in Bangor at an art opening and won't be home until late.

So maybe he fell asleep. Or his phone died. Or he noticed that his neighbors' house was on fire and had to single-handedly pull them to safety. Or—the more likely answer—maybe he got dragged to some party on the beach and is currently living it up . . . and avoiding my calls. These things happen. I know this, and I also know the world doesn't revolve around me and my expectations, that there's so much I can't expect to control. But . . .

Jackson Glanville doesn't *flake*. That's the thing. In a way, I wish he would. He'd be a lot healthier for it. Happier, too. But perfectionism, his absolute commitment to doing everything he agrees to do and doing it better than anyone else ever could, well, it's an obsession with him. It's been this way the whole time we've known each other, and we met all the way back in second grade. That's the year my family returned to Cabot Cove from Ann Arbor and also the one in which my mom's diagnosis turned grim.

On the first day I showed up at my new school, our teacher had Jackson show me around, to help me feel comfortable in a place that didn't have a lot of kids who looked like me, with brown skin and my hair in braids. And while that might sound odd—the Christian white boy asked to play tour guide for a biracial girl from a family of lapsed churchgoers—I have to believe Ms. Nielsen knew what she was doing. That she understood Jackson would put his whole heart into taking care of me because Jackson put his whole heart into everything he did.

She might've known other things, too. Things I would come to learn near the end of my mother's life. During those final agonizing months, I was at Jackson's house almost daily. This freed up my dad to spend time at the hospital, or later, to coordinate with hospice care, and I'd needed Jackson then. But it wasn't long before I understood that our friendship went both ways. That Jackson needed me, too, and that he held sorrow of his own, a rare and lonely sort of misery.

Because even amid my own tragedy and unbearable loss, I knew, every day, that my parents loved me.

And Jackson's simply didn't.

× × ×

The beach. That's the logical place to look, and I start back down the stairs, taking them quick, two at a time, as a wild thrum beat of urgency takes hold of my nerves.

Have to find him. I have to find him.

Without warning, my knees buckle, feet sliding out from under me. With a squeal, I cling to the rail to keep from falling farther, from tumbling to my death. I'm safe but stunned, hands scraped, hip bruised, and I squeeze my eyes shut.

Will myself to stay calm.

A frigid gust of wind slurps up the hillside, pricking my ears with chill. I reach back with the realization my hood's come off. Pulling it up, cinching it tight, I hear a sharp *crack* come from somewhere behind me.

Startled, I turn and stare furtively into the forest. No mouse could've made that sound. Not even a roof rat.

"Hey!" I hear a voice shout. Followed by: "Wait, what're you *doing*?"

Scrambling to my feet, I dart back up the stairs toward the Hollow.

"Hello?" I call into the darkness. "Jackson? Is everything all right?"

No one answers, but my voice echoes off the tight thicket of trees, the knotted planks of the treehouse, before bouncing back at me in a way that leaves me dizzy.

"Jax?" I call out again. "Is that you?"

And then, there it is. Another sound. Only it's not coming from the Hollow or the treehouse, which hovers above me—silent and decaying—but from somewhere deeper, somewhere farther into the woods. I strain to listen. It's almost as if there are *two* voices now, but they've grown muffled.

More muted.

Switching on my phone's flashlight, I rocket forward, heading into the trees.

"Jackson!" I cry. "Where are you? Are you okay?"

My light bobs wildly, but rather than answering, the voices fade, move westward. I follow gamely, moving as fast as I can while still being able to track what's going on. It's not easy. My heavy breathing and crashing footsteps drown the distant voices, and I keep having to stop and reorient myself. But each time, I hear it again, picking up what can only be the sound of bodies pushing through brush, the faint rise and fall of conversation.

The trail narrows, curving along the ridgeline as branches *thwap* against my arms. Maine's coastal hills run thick with trees, but also brush and loose rock, and I stumble, over and over. Still, I keep going. I have no clue why Jackson would be out here, but the person I heard sounded as if they were in danger. Not to mention, like anyone who's grown up here, I've heard stories about these woods.

About who or what might be in them.

Ahead, the voices fade, and again, I pause. Leaning my weight on a small sapling, I reach to unzip my fleece, exposing my torso to the biting wind. This is a survival technique and not the paradoxical undressing thing you hear about. The shirt I've got on underneath is cotton and sweat-soaked. My only hope for warmth is finding a way to dry it.

Only now I don't hear anything.

Puzzled, I lean over the edge of the hillside with my phone and scan the landscape. Nothing's down there. No movement. No sound. Turning slowly, I gaze above, up toward the peak. All I see are trees—thick trunks and swaying branches. Straining farther, I spy a hint of the looming shadow and stone façade of Broadmoor Castle.

The silence stretches as newfound worries settle in. What if the sounds I've been following weren't real in the first place? Just tricks of the wind or my own fevered imagination. Or something else entirely.

A whimper escapes me.

Oh, Jackson.

I've failed you.

Then I jump, startled like a snowshoe hare, because I *do* hear something. Only it's not voices and it's coming from the opposite direction.

From *behind* me.

I whip around, muscles tensed, eyes darting, as I try parsing this new information. The sound intensifies, until finally, I place it. I'm hearing *footsteps*, heavy footsteps, along with breathing, this strange guttural grunt—*Guh! Guh! Guh!* Whoever's making these sounds, they're moving fast, cutting through brush and gaining ground.

They're also coming straight for me.

A jolt of horror scrabbles up my spine. All this time I thought *I* was doing the chasing, the following. But what if this wasn't the case? What if I've got this all wrong, and somehow I've walked into a trap? What if I'm the one being hunted?

This time, I don't call out for Jackson. Or anyone.

I turn.

And run.

4

THERE'S THIS RECURRING DREAM I have. In it, Jackson and I are young. Really young. Maybe eight or nine. My hair's in glossy French braids and his is overgrown, dark bangs flopping past his eyes. We're playing together in a field of wheat, bathed by a dappled burst of golden light. Nearby, in a pasture, two horses graze on clover, long tails whipping softly as flies hover and dive.

Drenched in our own Technicolor hue, Jax and I race and laugh and tumble after each other. He's taller than I am, but I'm wily in a way I can't put words to. I know where he's going to go even before he does, allowing me to duck from his grasp, before darting in, ducking low, and taking him out by his ankles. The limber corgi to his lumbering St. Bernard.

Behind us sways an old barn. I say *sway* because this is exactly what it's doing. The barn's ancient, built on a stone foundation set by hand. The frame's come loose where the stones have crumbled, and when the wind blows you can actually watch the structure rock back and forth. I've gotten used to it, this sense of perpetual motion, but when a sharp gust comes up, the barn gives off an ominous moan, and I can't help but stare.

"Who's that?" I ask as a chill comes over me. My hesitation gives Jax the opening he needs. His body collides with mine and we both go down. My eyes stay open, but I land hard on my back with the wind knocked out of me. I'm staring at an upside-down image of the swaying barn, and I'm unable to speak. I can't get words out.

"Hey, that's Grandpa!" Beside me, Jax scrambles to his feet. "Where do you think he's going?"

I'm still gasping for air as he takes off, heading for the barn. Everything in my line of sight remains flipped, but I'm suddenly panicked. I don't want him to go. I want to call him off and warn him that the person I saw wasn't his grandfather, whom I don't like and don't trust. Only I don't know who it was, and all I can do is watch in horror as an upside-down Jackson disappears into the swaying barn.

This is the point I come awake with my heart pounding, my mind racing, and a scream of terror scrabbling up my throat. Only I *still* can't move. Even though I'm no longer on Jackson's grandfather's farm. Even though I'm lying in the dark in my room in my very own bed.

My body refuses to respond.

Then, finally, after far too long, my limbs twitch and tremble, my eyes open, and my lungs heave with relief, sucking in the sweet night air. *Sleep paralysis*, Dr. Wingate calls it, and he says it's not unusual to experience it in times of stress. *It's not unusual*, but what he means is that it's also not usual, and this is part of the reason I see him so often and why I continue to have the diagnoses and problems that I do. Anxiety and stress are as intertwined in me as ambition and intellect and a dark love of mystery. I guess what I'm trying to say is that the panic and dread and helplessness I feel inside my waking dream are the same as what I feel right now, tearing through the Maine woods to escape a danger I can't see or even identify.

Lucky for me, I'm still fast.

Still wily.

My legs are in agony, my breath coming in short, hard gasps. I don't dare look back, but what I hear behind me is maddening—the relentless slapping of footfalls and heavy breathing—*Guh! Guh! Guh!*—that are growing closer.

And closer.

"Over here!" a voice shouts.

I lift my head and see a light. It's coming from above the ridgeline and shining down on me. Then I see more lights appear, all bobbing and dancing. They must be phones, I realize, or flashlights.

"Hurry!" a different voice calls, waving their arms, urging me forward, as my nostrils pick up a hint of wood smoke. Like a campfire.

Like salvation.

A ragged whimper escapes my throat as I bear down for one last burst of speed, abruptly abandoning the trail and tearing up the hillside toward what I hope is safety.

My entire body chafes with effort, but I make it, cresting the hill and hurtling straight into the firelit clearing. Immediately, someone grabs me. I shriek, writhe, but their arms hold tight.

"It's okay," a stranger's voice murmurs in my ear. "You're safe. I promise. I just don't want you running into the flames. Okay?"

"Let *go*!" I wriggle free and spin around, staring back down into the darkness I just came out of. "Where are they? Do you see them?"

"Who's *they*?" the grabbing person asks.

"No one's out there," another voice says.

"Is someone chasing you?"

This last inquiry's uttered in a girl's voice, which surprises me enough to look up. Three teenagers I don't recognize are staring back at me. Two boys and a girl.

Shaking my head, I clasp my hand over my mouth and bite back the urge to scream. The urge to turn and keep running and never stop. Calm down, I tell myself. These are Broadmoor students. Just a trio of rich kids who wouldn't know danger if it wasn't subtracted from their trust fund's bottom line. They're drinking Glenlivet, for God's sake, and one of the boys is smoking cloves.

"Is someone chasing you?" the girl asks again, and with a quavering exhale, I examine her more closely. She's my age, I'd guess. Maybe a little older. Tall, too, with a heavy mane of dark blond hair that spills past her shoulders. Wide brown eyes and soft ruddy cheeks cast her face with that ethereal sort of innocence I associate with great wealth. It's a privilege to look that fragile. To let the world know it can break you.

"It's okay," she says soothingly. "You're safe here."

I nod. While my body continues to tremble, the panic recedes. Moving my gaze from the girl to the closest boy—the one who grabbed me—I blink, confused. He looks *just* like her. Sure, his hair's shorter and he's a few inches taller. But other than that, he's got the same coloring, the same ruddy softness, that same cherubic innocence.

"You're not seeing things," the second boy cuts in, the one with the cloves. His voice is soft, but commanding. "They're twins. I'm Carlos, by the way, and I would like it on record that I'm not in any way blood-related to these Stepford freaks."

My head swivels to take in Carlos, who—true to his word—does not resemble the other two. Hanging back by the fire with a stick in his hands, he's all mystery and restraint, with warm brown skin, dark hair cut short, and eyes that give away nothing.

I take a trembling step toward him. "What did you say?"

He straightens up. "That they're twins?"

"Before that. You said nobody was out there. What did you mean?"

Carlos tilts his head. "Just what I said. You came running up here, all freaked out, but no one was chasing you. No one else is out there."

"But how can you know that?"

"Come." He beckons with one hand. "I'll show you."

Curiosity overriding my caution, I walk to where Carlos is standing on the high side of the fire. He's not as tall as the twins, but there's something more self-assured in his movements, in the way he carries himself.

"Look." Carlos crouches beside me, gently pulling me with him, and points down the hillside. From this angle and vantage point, there's a clear view of the moonlit ridgeline below.

"You really didn't see anyone?" I ask.

"Just you."

"But you're the one who called to me. You helped me."

"That's right."

"Why?"

His gaze softens. His voice does, too. "I thought you needed help. The way you were running, the sounds you made . . ."

I turn away, suddenly mortified.

"Stop scaring her," the boy twin scolds, coming up behind us. "Carlos is a total wreck with girls when he flirts. Believe me. I've seen it before. It's not pretty."

Flirting? "You're from Broadmoor, right?"

"Is it that obvious? Come on, sit down. Stay awhile." Flashing an angelic smile, the boy twin gestures for me to sit in one of their fancy camping chairs, an offer I accept gratefully. My bones ache and it's a relief to collapse into the seat, scoot it closer to the flames and fire warmth. Carlos mutters something about gathering more wood while slipping into the darkness, and the girl twin sidles up, eager as a cocker spaniel, to drape a heavy teal-and-gold tartan across my shoulders.

"You're shivering," she explains.

"Thank you."

"Want some?" She holds out the Glenlivet, but I shake my head. "I'm Leisl, by the way. My brother's Leif."

I can't contain my shock. "Leisl and Leif?"

Her already red cheeks redden more. "We kind of have Stepford parents."

"Well, I'm Bea," I say. "Short for Beatrice."

The girl curls into the chair next to mine, pulling her long thoroughbred legs beneath her. "I know who you are. You're related to that famous author. The mystery writer who solved all those crimes back in the eighties or whenever."

"How do you know that?" I ask.

"She knows a lot of things." Leif walks around to the other side of the fire, keeping downwind from the smoke. "Or she thinks she does. A real walking Wikipedia."

Leisl rolls her eyes. "Wikipedia's virtual, and only a literal clown would suggest it's capable of ambulatory movement."

"A *literal* clown?"

"I said what I said." She turns her attention back to me. "Whenever I travel to new places, I like to know who the local celebrities are. In case I ever run into them, you know? Anyway, there's a photo of you on her website. Do you solve mysteries, too?"

"Not exactly," I say. "And someone *was* following me. Even if you didn't see them."

"Who?" Leif asks.

"I don't know. But I was at the Hollow earlier, waiting to meet a friend, only he didn't show, and I heard something in the woods. I thought it might be him, so I headed out on the ridge trail, but . . ."

"But what?"

I bite my lip. "I got turned around, I guess. Because suddenly whoever I was following was coming after *me*. Or maybe it was someone else. I don't know. I just started running, trying to lose them, and I ended up here."

"Lucky you," Leif says.

"What's your friend's name?" Carlos asks, having returned from the woods with an armful of sticks that he sets neatly on the ground.

"Jackson Glanville." I fumble for my phone. "Want to see a picture?"

They huddle close once I've got the photo up on the screen, but Leisl's the boldest. She plucks my phone out of my hands, holding it to her face and inspecting the image while simultaneously blocking her brother from shouldering in to get a peek.

Eventually the photo's passed around, but their response to it is strange. Hard to read. First off, I'm not sure I get the dynamic between Carlos and the twins. In my experience, friendships are rarely balanced, and most require a complicated push-pull of loyalty and one-upmanship in order to maintain. It's a game I'm admittedly lousy at, which is the reason I don't have a lot of close friends.

Other than Jackson.

Only nothing's off balance here. The bickering and teasing among these three feels good-spirited, like they're a well-oiled team, and their response to Jackson's photo is no different. It elicits a series of shared glances and knowing nods, a live current of interest. I even watch as Carlos forwards the photo to his own phone. Without *asking*.

"Hey, give me that." I reach to snatch my phone back.

"He's pretty hot," Leisl says with a smirk. "So where'd you get it?"

"Get what?"

"The photo."

"I took it."

"Off Facebook? Or one of the stock photo sites?"

"I took it at our high school," I say slowly. "In front of the chemistry lab."

"Hold up." Carlos lifts a hand and stares down at his phone while pacing the far side of the fire ring. "This might actually be a real image. At least, it's not coming up on any reverse image search."

"Why would it not be real?" I ask.

Liesl throws her head back and laughs, what would be a bright and joyful sound if I had any idea what it was she found to be so funny. "You don't have to pretend with us. I mean, you've been great and all. You really sold it with your whole 'I'm being chased' deal and that wild entrance. But you've got us. We're in. Let's do this."

I stare at her. "What?"

Carlos's brow furrows. "Guys, I'm thinking maybe she's not—"

"I've got it!" Leif cuts him off, turning to his sister with this wide Cheshire cat grin sprawling across his pale face. "You're thinking it's the missing friend thing, don't you?"

She nods, her intensity matching his. There's no more jokiness in their words, the body language they share. "First, the friend doesn't show up. Then she hears the commotion in the woods. Ends up getting chased. What're our options?"

"Could be a trap," Leif offers.

"Or a kidnapping."

"Or a *murder*!" He rubs his hands together and laughs gleefully.

"Stop it!" I shout, leaping to my feet and overturning my chair in the process. "If you can't help me find Jackson, that's fine. But I won't sit here and listen to you laugh about my friend possibly being *murdered*. It's beyond sick!"

There's a beat of stunned silence, then Carlos mutters, "I tried telling you. You two never listen."

Leif snorts. "For good reason."

"Enough." Carlos walks over to me, his brown eyes soft with remorse. "Bea, I am so sorry. I think that we've made a terrible mistake, and I sincerely apologize on behalf of all of us. We didn't mean to minimize your worry about Jackson, and I really hope he's okay. We all do, right?"

Leisl nods, but Leif folds his arms, lifts his chin. "I'm supposed to just believe her being here is a *coincidence*?"

"Maybe it is," Leisl says brightly.

"There's no such thing," he scoffs.

"Thanks, QAnon."

"That's *not* QAnon."

"*X-Files*?"

Leif sneers. "Try destiny."

I look Carlos in the eye. "I want you to tell me what's happening. Right now. Explain to me what they're talking about."

He gives a sheepish shrug. "I mean, it's not the worst conclusion we've ever come to. You're practically a detective. So it fits. It really fits."

"Fits *what*?" My jaw tightens. "Noncircular answers only."

A hush falls over the clearing as I hold Carlos's gaze to mine.

"Tenace," he says at last.

"Tennis?"

"Tenace," Leisl calls from her chair, kicking her legs up and cupping her hands around her mouth. "T-E-N-A-C-E."

"What is that?" I ask, and this is when I realize that Carlos is watching me. Very closely.

But why?

"You've never heard of it?" he asks.

"Should I have?" I pause. "Wait, is that Latin?"

"French," he says. "And tenace is a game. A very secret one. Sort of a Broadmoor tradition."

"You're all playing a *game*?"

"That's right. And these two"—Carlos hooks his thumb back at the twins—"think you're a part of it."

5

"I'D BETTER GO," I SAY because nothing about this night makes sense or makes me feel good about the people I've met and the choices I've made. Not to mention exhaustion and stress are catching up with me. They always do and every part of me aches.

"Where to?" Leisl asks.

Unsure how it's any of her business, I answer honestly. "Home, probably. Or maybe the beach. Jackson might be at the Cove. Tonight's homecoming."

"Gross," she replies.

Carlos is still looking at me. "What about the treehouse? Or back to the Hollow? Isn't that where you were supposed to meet? Maybe you could check there?"

"Maybe," I say. Had I mentioned the treehouse?

"She can't walk back the way she came," Leif calls out. "Not if she thinks someone was following her."

"Couldn't we walk her back?" Carlos asks.

"That'll take *forever.*"

Leisl brightens. "I know! We could walk you up to campus. It's not far and there's a shuttle that goes into town."

"Does it run this late?" I ask.

"No, it does not," Leif says.

"Then borrow Colby's car," Leisl tells him before turning back to me. "That's his roommate. He always lets Leif drive it."

"Don't you have a curfew?" I ask.

Leif shrugs. "Colby'll vouch for me. No one'll notice a thing, seeing as they haven't gotten around to installing our tracking chips yet."

"Sounds like a system ripe for abuse."

"Best thing about it," he says with a grin. "Plus, you can trust me. I'm totally sober. Unlike these two slobs."

"Thank you," I say, without acknowledging my surprise. "A ride would be great."

But no one moves.

"Maybe you should put the fire out," I offer.

Carlos nods. "I've got water for that."

Still, they don't move, not to get the water or gather up their belongings or anything. I stand there, waiting, but as the seconds tick away, I start to understand what's going on. I can feel that current of conspiratorial energy, arcing around the clearing. It's in the gleam in their eyes. The twitch of their lips.

Finally, I relent. "This is still about the game, isn't it?"

"Oh, *please*." Leisl clasps her hands together. "We just need your help with this one clue. Then we'll take you home. Promise."

"Jesus, Leis," Leif snaps. "It's not a hostage situation. It's a favor."

"I didn't *say* it was a—"

"Enough." I bark. "I'll help you. It's fine. I owe you that. Just tell me what you need, and we'll get it over with."

Leisl bounds over to give me a hug, then pulls the tartan tighter around me. "You're so cold," she whispers before stepping back as Leif gestures with a get-on-with-it motion.

I turn to Carlos. "Why don't you start by telling me what this game is about."

"Tenace," he corrects.

"Okay, tenace."

"Well, it's pretty simple. You know Broadmoor, right?"

"Yes, I know Broadmoor."

"Well, then, maybe you also know that most boarding schools, at least the ones here in New England, have secrets. Rituals, you could call them. Or traditions. They span a pretty broad range of activities. Some quirky; some fun or inspiring; some that walk the line toward hazing—looking at you, Choate Hall—but tenace is ours. It's played once every four years, and the mythology around it is hard to explain because it's so engrained in what Broadmoor is. Also, everything about it is meant to be secret. We take vows not to share it with outsiders, but . . ."

"But what?" I ask.

"The rules are complex. They're also open to interpretation. But the basic concept is that tenace is like an elaborate treasure hunt where you have to solve real-life puzzles and clues that will lead you to the next challenge. Only you never know what other players are doing or if they're on your side or not, which is where most of the strategy comes in and what makes the game so memorable."

"What strategy is that?" I ask.

"Bad faith," Leif says. "It's the foundation of all game play."

"Assuming bad faith or acting in it?"

"Either or."

"How do you win?" I ask.

"No one knows," Leisl says. "After every cycle of game play, a final ceremony is held in the spring out on Fiddler's Island for the winner. But what the prize is—if there even is a prize—or how it's earned is unknown."

"There's definitely a prize," Leif insists. "It's in the rule book."

"'Whomever shall be deemed the winner will be granted a prize of significant financial, emotional, and spiritual value.'" Carlos recites this from memory.

"There's a rule book?" I ask.

"An unofficial one. Something students have put together over the years."

"Then it could be filled with lies," I say. "Bad faith and all."

"Could be," he acknowledges.

"What do *you* think the prize is?"

Carlos shrugs. "There are plenty of rumors. That it's money. Or acceptance into the Ivy of one's choice. Maybe entry into a secret society so secret we've never heard about it. You hear other stuff, too. Like it's a government PSYOP or a recruiting tool for the CIA or even alien intelligence."

"Alien intelligence?"

"Look, none of that stuff makes sense. They're just

rumors. Maybe intentional misdirection. But at the end of the day everyone wants to win to prove they can."

"So you're playing for bragging rights."

Leif grins. "I mean, money wouldn't hurt. Some people's trust funds don't kick in until later in life."

"Some people?"

"I'm sure Carlos here probably wouldn't mind a little unfair advantage when it comes to college app time, and God knows what my sister wants out of it. But the real challenge lies in having to solve complex clues while navigating relationships in a scenario where it doesn't pay to be truthful. Or help others. Or even follow the rules."

"Outwit. Outplay. Outlast?" I say wryly.

"No." Carlos looks embarrassed. "It's not like that."

"Does the winner fall off a cliff onto an air cushion where everyone's waiting with champagne and balloons?"

"What?"

"She's talking about *The Game*," Leif says irritably. "And no. Come on, you're making it sound trivial."

I sniff. "You're the one who thought I might somehow be a part of it."

"But you *could* be." Leif walks toward me, his pale eyes glittering. "You admitted not knowing who was chasing you. And yet you ended up here. With us. Not to mention, you're a detective. Or—detective adjacent. I don't think that's random. Nothing about tenace is."

"I'm definitely not a detective," I say.

"That's not the point. You're meant to be here and you are. *That's* what this is about."

"Destiny?" I offer.

"I can think of other words."

My hackles raise. "So you think I'm acting? Or that I'm lying about my friend for a game I've never heard of? That's beyond insulting, to think the rest of the world cares about you so much that we're all just staging scenes for you to star in."

"Or maybe your life is just that insignificant," he snaps. "And you don't even know it."

"Leif," Carlos warns. "You're scaring her."

The thing is, I'm *not* scared. Not of Leif, at least. But his words send my mind spinning, churning through the implications of what he's saying.

Of what it might mean.

"Tell me the clue," I say quickly. "The one you're stuck on. I'll help as best I can."

With a terse nod, Leif pulls out his own phone and scrolls for a few seconds before finding what he's looking for. He reads aloud:

From the Badlands' evil harvest,
To a bloody Southern parish.
When the righteous choose depravity,
To invoke nonexistent supremacy.
To whom will the lawless answer?
For whom will their sovereign bell toll?

"That's it?" I ask when he's done. "That's the whole riddle?"

"Yeah."

"Well, that's easy. It's a posse comitatus."

"A what?"

"It was a right-wing anti-government movement in the seventies. People who revolted against paying taxes because they didn't want their money going to anyone not white or not Christian."

Leif scratches his chin. "I've heard that phrase—*posse comitatus*. But I thought it had to do with a federal act from 1878 barring the US military from acting as domestic law enforcement."

"That's true," I say. "But that's not what the clue you read is referring to. It's talking about a specific movement that took hold in rural areas. Followers formed militias and terrorized local law enforcement, all while claiming they were the ultimate arbiters of justice—a posse comitatus."

"How do you know all that?" he asks.

"*Evil Harvest*," I say. "It's a true crime book. Have you read it?"

"No."

"It documents the origins of an extremist religious group linked to the movement back in the seventies and eighties. They lived on a commune in Nebraska, hoarded guns, and claimed to be following God's law. The group ended up killing two people, including a child, and the way they did it—well, it's, uh, beyond dark. One of the more gruesome things I've ever read. And I've read a lot of true crime."

"What about the bloody Southern parish? What's that a reference to?"

"Probably the St. John the Baptist Parish ambush. A couple of deputies were shot down in Louisiana. That was more recent, though. Guess these people are still around."

A flash of irritation clouds his face. "You *guess*?"

Carlos jumps in by giving a low whistle and clapping his hands. "I'd say that's pretty damn impressive, Beatrice Fletcher. I think we've found our new walking Wikipedia."

"In the true crime category," I amend.

"Indeed." He smiles warmly, an odd contrast compared to Leif's surliness and Leisl's silence. *Are they out of sync now*, I wonder.

Or are they playing me?

"What's next?" I ask, but before Carlos can answer, Leif dumps the bucket of water directly onto the fire. Hissing plumes of gray smoke and steam fill the air, stinging my eyes, my nose, and sending Leisl into a coughing fit.

"I'm taking you home," Leif says when the smoke clears. "*That's* what happens next."

6

SATURDAY MORNING. THE SUNRISE BARRELS through my bedroom window with all the subtlety and grace of the Kool-Aid man.

I groan and curse past me for not closing the curtains, but when I try and pull blankets over my head I nearly gag. It's my hair. It smells *awful*—those noxious campfire fumes—and then the whole night comes rushing back. Jackson. The woods. Carlos and the twins. Their weird game and even weirder suspicions about my motives.

I yank the blankets back and sit up.

Jackson.

My phone's on my desk, charging. I reach to grab it and scan my messages. Nothing new, unfortunately, and nothing from him. They're all from last night, but from other folks, the ones who were urging me to come out. I've read them already, but in the light of day I carefully go over each message again, hoping to find something I missed.

Where are you B????

A sea monster just bit someone. I swear to god.

Beatttricccceeeeee get over here girl

nicki villanova lost her damn pants

This night is wild

Not even a *mention* of Jackson. A sob builds in my throat. I hadn't gone to the bonfire—the beach party had already broken up by midnight—but I'd done what I could last night after Leif dropped me off. I stayed up scrolling through photos on social media, calling hospitals, listening to the state police scanner, and scouring the TrueMaine database and forums for any news of accidents or acts of God.

There was nothing. No sign of him anywhere.

Throwing my phone down, I bury my face in my cat Lemon's long fur. She always sleeps at the foot of my bed. Feeling me press against her, she rolls over to show her tummy. I scratch her chin, rub her paws.

"Where is he, girl?" I whisper. "Where has he gone?"

× × ×

Ten minutes later, I swallow my Paxil while staring at myself in the bathroom mirror. My shrink's always telling me to *externalize my anxiety*, which I guess means to talk about it in a way that doesn't imply it's a fundamental part of who I am. I understand what he's getting at, but I don't know if I agree with the approach. Anxiety feels pretty fundamental to my overall personality structure, and so I tell myself that being wired for vigilance is my superpower. It keeps me attuned to every whiff of wrongness in the world. Every hint of despair.

So then why am I taking the pills?

I turn away, beyond irritated with my own illogical thought patterns, and focus on getting ready. Once showered and dressed, I go downstairs and find my father's already there. Standing in our cozy nook of a kitchen with a mug of coffee clutched in his grasp and his angular face coated in pinky sunrise light streaming through the back slider, he looks more exhausted than I feel. He's also dressed up. Sort of. He's currently sporting a wrinkled button-down shirt, khakis, and a loosely knotted tie, all of which are at odds with his usual appearance—what I lovingly call "nerdy Indiana Jones." Or alternatively, "hipster Ichabod Crane."

"Hi, Daddy," I say. "You do know it's Saturday, don't you?"

He smiles, but his response is slow. "Hey, sweetie. There's more coffee on, if you want it."

"Are you going somewhere?" On Saturdays, we usually cook breakfast together. My plan was to use this time to ask for help with the Jackson situation.

But my father reaches to muss his already mussed hair and offers me a sheepish nod. His eyes are bleary, red-rimmed, as if he hasn't slept, and it's an unsettling contrast with his usual sharp-eyed focus. "I have to be at work this morning. I'm sorry, Bea. I thought I'd mentioned it before."

"It's fine. Don't be sorry." I pause, hoping he'll say more and keep the conversation going.

Instead, he turns and dumps the rest of his coffee into the sink before sliding the mug into the dishwasher.

"Why do you have to be there on a weekend?" I finally ask.

He uses a dishrag to wipe down the butcher block counter. "We're still down an analyst and the lab's going through these upgrades. Lot of equipment coming in today. I just . . . I need to be there. Inventory was off in the last shipment and that can't happen again. Not with the time frame I'm working under."

"It's fine," I say again.

Dad squeezes my shoulder and kisses my cheek. His chin's rough, dotted with salt-and-pepper stubble, and I can tell his thoughts are as choppy as my own. He recently became the lead on a new development project at Bio-Mar—something something environmental contagion detection—and as a man who's watched the love of his life wither and die from an illness she had no genetic predisposition for, his work—his purpose in life—is deeply personal.

"What're you doing up so early?" He reaches for his truck keys. "Anything going on that I should know about?"

"No, Daddy," I say brightly, my heart hardening a little with the lie. But it wouldn't be fair to burden him more when he's already so worn down. "Nothing's going on. I hope you have a good day."

He leaves, and I follow shortly after. Like father, like daughter, I guess. We're both easily consumed, and we keep things to ourselves. And with this searing insight, I step out onto the front porch, grab my bike from the rack, slip my helmet on, top off the tires, and go.

7

Outside, everything's coated in frost, a soft dusting of death. Once on the street, I pedal gingerly at first, my muscles sore and stiff from the previous night.

Rolling easy, tires crunching on leaves, I take in the view, and this neighborhood never fails to thrill me. On both sides of the street, neat rows of stately trees shudder and brim with fall color. The homes, a sprawling mix of well-kept Victorians and shaggy Colonials, are likewise in a festive mood—many adorned with pumpkins, gourds, corn husks, and an eclectic mix of store-bought skeletons, arched cats, looming spiders, witches, ghosts, and graveyards.

Muscles warmed, I pick up speed, coasting down asphalt and turning onto the main road for the ride out toward Seacrest. This is where the Glanvilles live. It's also where they rule—this past February, Jackson's mother won a hard-fought reelection bid for president of the insufferable Seacrest Homeowners Association Board and won't let anyone forget it.

Seacrest, by the way, is our town's oldest and wealthiest enclave. Running along the cove's less windy south side, most of the homes here have been designated as having historical significance. Just driving through the community's five-mile waterfront stretch to gawk at a few dozen gaudy mansions has recently become a favorite tourist attraction. Oh, and doing so costs money these days. Upward of eight dollars, if I remember correctly.

Well, Cabot Cove's non-Seacrest residents are exempt from the fee, but we still have to check in at the main gate. Private security actually patrols the streets around here, so if you're not on the list—and especially if you're not white—God help you. Squeezing the bike's brakes and setting a foot down, I pull up to the guardhouse window, knock sharply, and squint to see who's working.

The broad-shouldered shaggy-haired person inside slides open the window. "Hey, Bea."

I smile shyly. It's Andy Fuchs, who I really like. A local college student, Andy's a couple years older than me, but our fathers work together at Bio-Mar, so we've socialized before at cookouts and clambakes and even a backpacking trip to Nova Scotia last summer. This morning he's bundled in a thick navy parka, has a space heater blasting at his feet, and he's gripping a to-go cup from the local café as he reads a book that's spread open on the plywood guardhouse desk.

I nod at the paperback. "What is that?"

He holds it up. The book's slim and worn and it's got the word *spider* in the title.

"Is it for a class?" I ask.

"Cinema and literature in post-fascist Italy."

"Are you liking it?"

"So far. You heading out to the Glanvilles this morning? Kind of early, isn't it?"

"It is," I acknowledge. "Hey, have you seen Jackson at all? Either coming or going?"

Andy scratches his chin. "My shift started at six. I pretty much just got here. Why're you asking?"

"I couldn't reach him last night. We had plans to meet, but he never showed."

"Meet where?"

"The Hollow."

Andy frowns. "Come on, Bea. Don't go out there. Especially not alone. That place is seriously cursed."

"Cursed?"

"I know you've heard the stories. Weird glowing orbs hovering in the air. Lots of people have seen them."

"Do you mean flashlights?"

He rolls his eyes. "Didn't some Broadmoor chick die out there last year?"

"That was somewhere else," I say. "Out near Lake Paloma. I actually helped look for her when she went missing. Or, I tried to. Our group was kind of a failure."

"Of *course* you joined a search party. You're the most social introvert I know."

I ignore this. "Turned out she fell while hiking."

"That's not what I heard," Andy says.

But before I can coax him into telling me what he's

heard, a shiny town car pulls up behind me and the driver flashes their lights. Andy lifts a hand, then opens the gate. Waves me through.

"Thanks," I say, pushing off on my bike and wobbling a little down the road.

"Be careful," he yells. "And stay out of the woods."

× × ×

Stay out of the woods.

Andy's warning lingers. I don't care for scolding, but he's right. Regardless of where the Broadmoor girl died, there have long been warnings and stories about who or what might be prowling in the woods above town. Plenty of people swear they've seen ghosts and floating lights and yetis and fae creatures out there. It's usually tourists who share these stories, and there's not much harm in letting them create a sense of shared lore and mystery around the town. Fear's one of our state's top exports, after all, which is what TrueMaine's trying to capitalize on. And for the record, while our countryside is reportedly rife with lake monsters and cloven-hooved goat men, my favorite legend has always been the mist. That cool coiling vapor with the power to surround you, to take over your mind.

That same vapor's currently blowing off the ocean, swirling around my feet as I pedal. It's another quarter mile before I turn onto White Cap Court, which consists of precisely three homes. The Glanvilles' is at the very end, perched atop a woolly bluff, overlooking the ocean.

Coasting to a stop at the base of their cobblestone

driveway, I slide from my bike and stare up at this house that contains so many of my childhood memories. Few of them good. In both structure and sensibility, the Glanville house towers gloriously, thrust over the sea like a stand against nature. Or Ahab to his whale. Officially listed in the Cabot Cove Historical Society as the "Wright House," after Mrs. Glanville's family, the structure boasts three gothic stories crafted from stone and glass. When winter descends in all its frostbit glory, being inside the house is like being trapped within a snow globe, but a warm one with all its six working fireplaces burning madly to fill the rooms with heat.

But a darker force lurks within these walls. It's hard to explain, but I believe certain personalities generate certain sorts of energy. Certain places do, too, and I've witnessed it, the cruel alchemy that comes alive inside this home when Jackson gets around his parents. Especially his father. It's like instinctually, he can't stand to be around his own son. Only instead of rejecting him, Deacon Glanville's convinced himself that destroying everything good about Jackson is what God put him on this earth to do.

The way Jax tells it, it started with strict rules and a demand for perfect compliance. At all times. Not to mention, from a young age, his appearance has been an obsession for his parents, which is weird considering Jackson is way better looking than either of them. Well, physically, his mom's fine, I guess, in a rich-woman way. But the deacon's sort of hunched and balding, with a complexion and coloring best described as "beige." Anyway, from early on, they've acted like the mere sight of Jackson was a moral offense, forever fussing about dirt on his face, whether he had too many freckles, and whether he'd washed his hair or brushed his teeth, even if they'd seen him do both. Jackson had a stink to him, too, they said, and it wasn't like other kids. He had to see doctors and use medicated soap, medicated shampoo, and medicinal mouthwash multiple times a day. Likewise, his clothes had to be clean, unwrinkled, and always tasteful, although the standard for good taste was unspoken and everchanging. And so it went, on and on and on, and the only consistency was Jackson's inevitable failure, although even his parents' response to such failure failed to be consistent. At times his father would fly into a seething rage, and at others, he and his wife would simply ignore Jackson's presence for days on end. They would just move through their home and routine as if their child were a ghost. Or better yet, as if he'd never been born.

Nothing's changed much since then, except the standards and expectations put upon Jackson have been raised and the technology they use to track his movements has grown more sophisticated. I've long tried to make sense of this. How anyone could justify forcing a child to suffer in the name of conformity.

War may be partly to blame; Deacon Glanville enlisted in the Army after 9/11 and was deployed to Afghanistan three times before returning home to his wife and young son and joining the ministry. But based on what I know of him, I'd say his real issues lie further in the past, somewhere in his own childhood and sordid upbringing.

You see, the dream I have about Jackson's grandfather's horse farm is based on real events. Years ago, Jax and I were sent to spend a week there over the summer, up in the northwestern part of the state. And while nothing terrible happened to me personally, the same can't be said for Jackson. His grandfather, a once-renowned horse trainer, had clearly resented our presence, alternating between fits of open hostility and outright negligence. Eager to stay out of his way, Jax and I visited a widowed neighbor woman with some frequency. She fed us oatmeal cookies and watered-down punch in her lime-green kitchen that was crowded with racist knickknacks ("my collection" she'd said proudly, after assuring me her mammy figurines and Sambo cookie jars weren't offensive).

On our second to last morning on the farm, a bee stung my neck as Jackson and I played along the banks of a quiet frog-filled pond. The wound swelled fast, red and hot to touch. Fearful, Jackson sprinted to find his grandfather, disappearing into the gently swaying barn. Just like in my dream.

I heard what happened before I saw the evidence. When Jackson returned, his nose was bloody, his lip cut, and his shirt torn.

There was also a dark fury simmering in his blue eyes.

Jackson wouldn't tell me what had happened, but I knew it was violent and bad, and so I ran, fast as I could, to the widow's house. When I found her, I threw myself at her mercy, begging her to call my father. To call anyone who would take us home.

Which she did.

Yeah, well, talk about cursed places: The following summer, the FBI raided Jackson's grandfather's farm and took him into custody. Turned out he was the sole suspect in a series of unsolved package bomb and booby trap attacks targeting individuals he'd believed to be involved in secret government experiments and other abuses of power. Mostly conspiracy theory–type stuff from the sixties and seventies. Things I'd never heard of and probably weren't true. Like the government spraying infectious bacteria over a major US city. Or a college in the Midwest conducting an experiment in which small children undergoing speech therapy were purposely shamed and ridiculed by their teachers in order to measure the effect. Only, unlike the Unabomber, who'd lived alone and off the grid while mailing explosives and writing his manifesto on the ills of technology, Jackson H. Glanville, aka the Jack in the Box Bomber, had allegedly planned and executed his crimes—which led to a total of seven deaths and numerous injuries—all while breeding his prized thoroughbreds and raising a family, including his own son.

He'd also died in federal detention two months later while

awaiting trial. Heart attack, apparently. Everyone in Cabot Cove agreed this was "for the best," since coverage of the trial would've been torturous for the family. Jackson's father—now known as Deacon Glanville—publicly denounced Glanville Sr., but that hadn't kept him from being harassed and having to step back from his duties at the parish. It was during this time that I overheard my uncle telling my dad that now they knew the reason Deacon Glanville was so screwed up. My ears perked up at this, but they both quieted when they saw I was in the room. And I'd hated that, even then. The way adults lie and deflect when they fear children learning the truth about a world we already know is unjust.

So, no, I'm not privy to any of the details, but it's not a stretch to believe that growing up with a serial killer might have scrambled Deacon Glanville's understanding of fatherhood. Even if he'd had no idea about his father's crimes, his own anger and need for control hint at earlier darkness. Maybe he'd endured his own split lip and bloodied nose. But then why would he name his only child after his father?

And why send us to the horse farm that summer?

These are questions I'll never have answers to. And although I can have pity for what young Deacon Glanville might've gone through as a child, I find him terrifying as an adult. Multiple reasons have led me to avoid this house over the past few years, but fear has always been at the top.

Fear's also what holds me in its grip as I stand in the street, desperate to find the courage to walk to the front door, ring the bell, and ask the Glanvilles where their son might be.

Baby steps, my mind whispers, and I start by carefully laying my bike down, handlebars on the sidewalk, wheels in the street. The likelihood of someone calling security because I've broken some unknowable Seacrest rule on bike placement is high, so I'm hedging my bets here. What I know *not* to do, however, is push the bike onto the Glanvilles' property, where I would undoubtedly be on the receiving end of a nasty lecture, along with multiple accusations of property damage.

Next, I walk through the aggressively landscaped front yard and onto the porch. An ivy-draped arbor shelters the doorway, but through arched side windows and gauzy silk drapes, I'm able to catch a glimpse into the Glanvilles' breakfast nook. There's a figure moving around in there. Too shadowy to make out, but I have no doubt it's Jackson's mother.

My breath goes ragged as I envision what comes next. How the door will open and I'll be face-to-face with an aging beauty queen who sees me as trouble, at best, and an active saboteur in her son's future success, at worst. How I'll stammer and sweat and attempt to justify my presence under the weight of her withering stare that seeks to catalog my every character flaw. My every move.

Still, I'm reaching for the doorbell when a man's voice calls out, "Marla! What was that? Did you hear something? I think someone's at the door."

Oh God. Before I even know what I'm doing, I leap back and scramble off the slate porch in a flurry of cowardly

8

HALF EXPECTING TO HEAR SIRENS or shotgun blasts erupting in the air behind me, I race out of Seacrest and back into the main road. Once I'm safely out of the private security firm's jurisdiction, I pull to the side of the road and call Jackson.

Straight to voice mail. I leave a garbled apology about stopping by his house but not wanting to get him in trouble with his folks. The whole thing's a mess, I say, but he should call me whenever he gets this. Like, immediately.

Please.

Unsure of what to do next, I hop back on my bike's fraying seat and I just keep riding, keep moving. Pedaling into town, I soon find Cabot Cove's got signs of life. A line of cars is already heading toward the beach, and a handful of families have gathered to watch a kite exhibition that's setting up by the waterfront. The whole thing's so painfully wholesome that I'm almost physically sick. How can life and beauty and mundane pleasures just go on when someone as wonderful as Jackson is missing?

They will, though. That's the thing. People talk about the butterfly effect and the interconnectedness of the universe, but I've never known any of that to be true. Your whole world can implode and nothing around you will change, not in any meaningful way.

Gritting my teeth, I resist the urge to spiral into self-loathing. I have to do something to make up for my cowardice back at the Glanville house. Finally, I decide to try what I should've last night: going to the Cabot Cove Sheriff's Office and explaining what's happened.

This might sound easy and it probably should be, but by the time I get there, all the way on the far side of town, I'm a total wreck. My legs are trembling, my stomach's sour, and there's this frantic voice inside my head warning me that this whole idea is *dangerous, reckless, very bad, terrible.*

Well, now I'm not sure if my anxiety's a superpower or a villain, but I'm here and I push through the station's double doors and walk inside. I clear the lobby's metal detector, which makes me feel guilty for reasons best explored in therapy, and march up to the front desk.

"I need to talk to someone," I say to the young woman seated behind a bulletproof partition. This feels like overkill in a town this size, but the entire sheriff's office was rebuilt last year on account of black mold, and an effort's been made to erase the folksy down-home atmosphere of the old one. A mistake, in my opinion. The new building's all design forward with sleek surfaces and a metallic color palette, and the end result is that it resembles a remodeled McDonald's more than anything else.

"What's that?" the woman barks. "I can't hear you. Speak up."

My throat tightens. *Speak up* is just about my least favorite phrase in the English language. Still, I do my best and repeat my request.

"What's this in reference to?" she asks.

"It's about a friend of mine. He's missing. Or . . . I can't find him, and I'm worried something might've happened."

"Like what?"

"I don't know exactly. It's just, he's not anywhere. And it's not like him."

"How old is he?"

"Sixteen." Sudden panic comes over me. "I'm not supposed to wait twenty-four hours, am I?"

"That's only for adults." The woman takes my name and asks me to wait. I spend the next ten minutes pacing the lobby and staring at the bulletin board's pinned announcements on water safety, snow blowing tips, and Have You Seen Me? photos of missing children. There are a ton of these, which is depressing, and some stretch back for years with computer-enhanced age-progression photos printed beside younger ones. Even more depressing, I actually recognize a couple of the names, kids I've gone to school with. The accompanying photos of them are surreal in a way that's hard to explain, and even the thought that Jackson could be up here, too, is enough to leave me light-headed.

I *hate* this.

"Beatrice Fletcher?"

I turn and see a tall woman with a mass of frizzy dark hair standing by an open door. She's wearing a beige pantsuit—not a CCSD deputy uniform—and gestures for me to come over. My mouth goes dry, but I oblige, and as I'm walking over, my phone buzzes in my pocket. Reaching to pull it out, I can't help but believe it's him, that he's texting me, that everything's fine and this is over, and I can turn around and get out of here. But when I look at the message, it's from *Carlos*.

Thanks again for your help last night.

Oh, and the twins say hi.

×××

"Sit down." Lieutenant Deputy Bernstein—this is what she tells me her name is—waves to a folding chair on the far side of her desk before settling into her own seat. We're not in a real office. It's more of an open cubicle-type area, which means anybody walking past can hear what we're saying.

I sit and realize I don't know what to do with my arms. Also my left knee starts jiggling.

"You're Frankie's kid, right?" Lt. Deputy Bernstein's got this gruff no-nonsense voice, but up close, her hair's kind of amazing. In addition to being super curly, it's streaked with gray, giving her a compelling Bride of Frankenstein vibe.

I straighten my spine. I know well enough to keep hair thoughts to myself. "How do you know my dad?"

"My brother was in the same class as him at CCH. Three years ahead of me," she says.

"Oh. That's cool."

"It was good to see him move back here. Most people don't do that."

"Don't do what?" I ask.

"Return to their roots." She clears her throat, pulls out a small laptop, and starts typing. "I hear you're worried about someone?"

"Yeah. A friend of mine. I can't find him. His name's Jackson Glanville. You, uh, probably grew up with his parents, too. Or his mom, at least."

"I know the family."

"Right." I feel flustered. I'm not sure what that means. "Well, Jackson and I had plans to meet up last night. Only he didn't show. I've tried calling him, texting. Checking in with mutual friends. But no one's heard anything. And I know it might sound like I'm being paranoid, but it's really out of character for him not to respond. He's not a partier. And he's super reliable. I just have this feeling that . . ."

"That what?" she asks.

My knee jiggles faster. "Something's wrong."

"Have you talked to his parents? Do you know if he's at home?"

"No."

"How old is Jackson?"

"Sixteen."

"Does he drive?"

"He's not allowed until he's twenty-one."

Lt. Deputy Bernstein lifts an eyebrow. "Says who?"

"His parents."

"And what's your relationship with Jackson?"

I shrug. "We're friends."

"Romantic friends?"

"No. It's nothing like that."

More typing. "Where were you and Jackson supposed to meet last night?"

"The Hollow."

"What time?"

"Eight forty-five. In the evening."

"And what was the purpose of this meeting? What were you going to do?"

Sweat beads on my forehead, right above my brow. "We were going to go to a therapy group. I've been trying to get him to go for a while now. I'd actually made special arrangements with the therapist to bring Jackson last night and introduce the two of them . . ."

Lt. Deputy Bernstein's head snaps up. "A therapy group? What, like a twelve-step thing?"

Twelve-step? "No, it's a teen support group."

"Who's this therapist?"

"His name's Dr. William Wingate. He's a psychiatrist, actually, who specializes in working with adolescents and young adults. He has a clinical practice in his home."

"His *home*?"

"Yes."

She grunts. "And last night, you were planning on introducing Jackson to this Dr. Wingate?"

"I was."

"So then why were you meeting at the Hollow?"

"It was a cover, you know? Saying we were there so that people wouldn't know where we were really going."

"Did Jackson's parents know you were taking him to a psychiatrist?"

Now the sweat beads start to roll, first cresting my brow before dipping down my nose. "Minors over the age of fourteen can consent to their own mental health treatment in the state of Maine."

"So that's a no?" she asks. "Figures. Can't imagine those parents of his would be too thrilled about this kind of scenario. They don't seem the type. What was Jackson seeking treatment for?"

"That's personal," I say. "You'd have to ask him."

Her response is to literally start pantomiming that she's looking around the room for someone, culminating in her pulling open a drawer and peering in there, which is beyond insulting. "How strange. I don't see Jackson anywhere. Considering that you're reporting him missing, I guess I can't ask him."

My cheeks blaze. "He just needed to talk with someone, all right? It was group therapy. A place to get support."

"So Jackson needs support?"

"Doesn't everyone?" I ask.

Lt. Deputy Bernstein shrugs. "Not everyone goes to therapy."

I feel a headache coming on. "Look, I don't know why this is so important. The point is that we never went to the group because he didn't show up. I'm just trying to find out where he is now, and I want to know he's safe. I'm worried something might've happened."

"Like what?"

"I don't know!" To my own ears, my voice sounds weak, pitiful even. "Isn't that your job to figure out? He's not the first teen to go missing in Cabot Cove, is he?"

Lt. Deputy Bernstein doesn't answer.

Sensing an opening, I keep going. "There's a whole bulletin board of missing kids in this very building. At least three people from my own school have vanished in the last eighteen months. And no one talks about it! There was even that girl from Broadmoor last spring. She went missing and when someone did find her, she was *dead*."

"You think there's a connection between these missing teens and your friend? Or the Broadmoor girl's death?"

"There could be! It's worth looking into. It's worth doing something!"

For a moment Lt. Deputy Bernstein doesn't reply. She's still typing into her laptop, and I don't know what she's documenting, but I also don't think I want to know.

At last, she looks up. "How would you describe Jackson's state of mind of late? Would you say he's suicidal? Or has he seemed despondent in recent days?"

I feel weak. I grip the arm of my chair. "Why're you asking me this?"

"These are standard questions."

"They don't sound like it."

Lt. Deputy Bernstein purses her lips. "Are you saying that Jackson Glanville's never talked to you about hurting himself or wanting to hurt himself?"

I force myself to speak slowly. "I'm saying none of that's relevant. Jackson wouldn't hurt himself so it's not worth talking about his personal life. These questions just seem like reasons for you to rationalize not doing anything to help him."

"Is that really what you believe?"

"It's really what it feels like," I snap.

"Well, I happen to find it interesting that you, of all people, would say something like that." Lt. Deputy Bernstein reaches into her desk drawer and pulls out a blue manila folder. "As you noted earlier, I *am* familiar with the Glanville family. This is due, in large part, to the fact that I was the responding officer on a missing person report filed two years ago regarding Jackson Glanville. A very *personal* report. I assume you know the one I'm referring to."

"Yes." My voice is basically a whisper.

"Good." She smiles. "That makes sense, obviously. Seeing as you were the one who filed it."

9

I'M SHAKING AS I STORM out of the Sheriff's Office and march away from the building under a cloud of rage. Because yes, *yes*, I did file that report back in eighth grade.

And I've paid dearly for it ever since.

Reaching my bike, I pull my phone out to call Jackson *again*, and a howl of rage escapes me as I realize the futility of it all. He's not going to answer, and I don't know why. I have no way of knowing why. I nearly fling the phone to the ground in frustration. What am I supposed to *do*? Why does caring about someone always end with loneliness and despair? It's a lesson I keep learning, yet more than ever, I crave closeness. I long for someone who will believe in me and what I love and won't judge me for finding beauty in the morbid.

For an instant, I consider calling my shrink. I mean, I should so that I can apologize for flaking last night. But also, maybe *he* could tell me how to fix things.

But that sense of shame.

It's so *strong*.

Instead, I pull up Carlos's earlier text and reply:

Hey, are you free?

×××

"Thanks for meeting with me." Forty minutes later, I've got a maple cardamom latte on the table in front of me, wafting its warm spicy goodness into my nostrils, and I'm sitting across from Carlos, who's joined me downtown at the crowded Main Street Café. "I didn't know who else I could talk with."

"I didn't realize we'd grown so close," he says. "Considering we only met last night."

"I don't remember using the word *close*."

Carlos smiles as he stirs his coffee, to which he's added a total of four creamers. "You didn't. But I am a little surprised to hear you don't have other friends in your life that you can talk to."

"I do have other friends . . ." I say, before trailing off because while that's true, Carlos's point still stands. I'm here with him in a time of need. Not them.

Why is that?

He leans forward over the thick oak tabletop, dark eyes meeting mine. "It's okay, Bea. This doesn't need to be complicated. It doesn't have to be anything. I was able to come and I'm here. And I really did enjoy meeting you last night. Odd circumstances notwithstanding."

"Thanks," I say, feeling both relieved and bashful. "It *was* odd, wasn't it?"

"Very. But you broke up the twins' bickering, so that can only be a good thing."

This makes me grin, in spite of my mood. "You all seem

so close. Like you've known each other forever. How did you meet?"

"It's pretty hard *not* to meet someone at Broadmoor. You'd have to work at it. But last year, Leisl was roommates with a girl I was seeing. So I got to know her—and by extension, Leif—pretty well. They're kind of inseparable."

"Fascinating," I say. "I don't have a sibling, much less a twin. Is that a normal thing—for fraternal twins to have that kind of closeness?"

Carlos lifts a brow. "They're not sleeping together, if that's what you're asking."

"No!" I'm horrified at the thought. "That is *not* what I'm asking."

"Good. They hate jokes like that. And believe me, they've heard them all. There's not a lot to do up at Broadmoor so everyone is in everyone else's business. It's all very high stakes."

"Where's the girlfriend?" I ask.

"What?"

"Leisl's roommate. You didn't think I'd skip that detail, did you?"

Carlos shakes his head and does more coffee stirring. "The girlfriend's not in the picture anymore. And Leisl has a new roommate this year."

"Sorry for being nosy," I tell him.

"It's fine."

"Well, it's your turn to ask a question," I say quickly.

He thinks about this for a moment, giving me time to study him more closely. In the warm café light, Carlos is handsome in that way where looking at him is both pleasing and nonthreatening. He's more than the sum of his parts, I guess. Individually, his ears are a little too big, his smile's on the toothy side, and his neck's got one of those bulging Adam's apples. But he exudes calmness and serenity in a way I certainly never do, and it somehow all works.

"Okay," he says at last. "Can I ask you something kind of serious?"

"Sure," I say.

"The friend you were looking for last night. Jackson. Have you found him?"

My chest knots. "Are you saying you actually believe he exists? That he's not just a character cast in your weird boarding school game?"

Carlos shoots an uneasy glance around the room. "No. I mean, *yes*, I believe he exists. Of course, I do. I'm sorry we ever doubted you."

I shake my head vigorously, suddenly filled with regret. Why am I like this? "It's okay. I'm sorry. I'm so sorry. I shouldn't have said that."

"Last night," he says. "That all must've been really confusing for you."

"It was."

"Then you have nothing to be sorry about, okay? That was on us. And it was unfair."

"Thank you." I wrap trembling hands around my drink. "And to, uh, answer your question—yes, he's still missing."

Carlos frowns. "How worried are you?"

"Very. I was at the Sheriff's Office right before I texted you. That's kind of why I needed someone to talk to. But don't worry. I didn't tell them anything about you guys or being in the woods."

"You didn't tell them that? Why not?"

I stare into my drink's foam. "I don't know. The detective didn't believe anything I was saying anyway. She thought I had something to do with his disappearance, when it's Jax's parents she should be worried about."

"His parents?"

"They're awful," I say.

"Like, abusive awful?"

"Not physically," I say slowly, not wanting to reveal too much. "It's hard to explain. If someone had told me emotional abuse could be just as damaging as physical abuse, I don't think I'd believe them if I hadn't seen the way Jackson's parents treat him. And maybe a different type of personality would do fine with that kind of parenting, but not him."

"You really care about him."

"I *do*," I say. "But it's complicated. This whole thing is complicated. And maybe that's why I'm talking to you instead of people who know us."

Carlos shakes his head. "I'm not following."

I hesitate. "Up until six months ago, Jackson Glanville hated me."

×××

Carlos rubs his smooth chin and sort of looks uncomfortable, like maybe he shouldn't have taken me up on my invitation for coffee after all. I don't blame him. Here we are, sitting in the back room of a local café. Everything's wood-paneled and cozy, the air rich with the scent of cinnamon and butter, the tables crowded with a mix of locals and tourists. He's shower fresh in jeans, a white T-shirt, and brown suede coat, and he probably assumed this was a date or something, and instead I'm burdening him with my darkest secrets.

The ones I can't bear to hold.

"I don't think I understand," he says at last. "Isn't Jackson your friend?"

"He *is*," I insist. "We've known each other for forever. He's the kindest, most warm-hearted person you'll meet. He took care of my cat once, when I was out of town, and by the time I got back, he'd knitted an entire blanket with her face on it. It's still her favorite."

"Lucky cat," Carlos says. "So he's your boyfriend?"

"No. That's never been a thing between us. We're more like the twins in that way. Except we're both only children."

"Okay . . ."

I try and catch Carlos's eye, to let him know I'm genuinely glad he's here and that it's not by accident or desperation that I invited him. "Look, two years ago, when we were in eighth grade, I did something that made Jackson angry with me. I thought it was the right thing to do at the time, and I guess I still think that. But what I did then is complicating what I do now, and I don't know what's right anymore."

"Tell me," he says.

"Well, first off, Jackson was basically my only friend in

Cabot Cove for a long time. My family moved here when I was seven and he was the first person to welcome me. I was kind of shy back then and my mom was sick with breast cancer, so he was all I had. And he never made me feel bad for that. Not even as we got older, and he got into other things like basketball and robotics and oceanography and all kinds of nerdy science stuff."

"Hey, some of us like that nerdy science stuff," Carlos says.

"But are you one of Maine's Top Twenty Young Science Scholars?" I ask. "Selected out of over two hundred applicants and guaranteed an in-state scholarship, should you choose to accept it?"

"No," he says. "I'm not. That's very impressive."

"It is. Kind of beyond comprehension, really. Anyway, one day, near the end of eighth grade, Jackson didn't show up at school. He also didn't answer his phone or texts. And there was nothing on social media. It was so abrupt. Finally, after doing everything I could think of to reach him, I called the Sheriff's Office and reported him missing. I told them I was worried about his safety and that I thought he might hurt himself."

Carlos stares at me intently. "Was that true?"

I nod. "He was in a bad place then. With his parents and home life. With being depressed but also being a perfectionist. He just held himself to these ridiculous standards and didn't believe it was right to burden people with his problems. More than once he'd told me that he thought about jumping off the North Minuet Bridge. Plus, I knew he'd done other things before that. Took pills. Tried cutting his wrists."

"Jesus."

"Thank God, the cops took me seriously. They sent a car to his house and when they didn't find him there, they went out looking for him and found him walking along the coastal highway after midnight, just south of the bridge. They ended up picking him up and taking him to an adolescent psychiatric facility where they held him for two weeks before his parents had him transferred to a private facility. He stopped talking to me after that."

"That's terrible," Carlos says. "But what happened six months ago?"

"He stopped being angry," I say. "One day he asked if we could talk, and we did and then all of a sudden we were friends again. Talking on the phone, meeting up to go on walks at night like we used to. He told me he forgave me and that he knew I wanted to help him. Which is also what I was trying to do last night."

"And now you think he might've tried to hurt himself again?" Carlos asks.

"No," I say. "That's just it. He wouldn't. Not when we had a plan in place to get him help. But no one believes me because of last time."

"Yeah, I don't know." Carlos looks uncomfortable. "People are good at hiding things. Especially perfectionists."

"I know that. I just—I don't know how to explain it. But he wouldn't hurt himself. I know it."

"Bea." Carlos leans closer, his elbows sliding across the table. "Did you ever think that the reason Jackson—"

"Beatrice!" I look up, right into the beaming face of Evie Ranier. Farther behind her, waiting for drinks, I also spot Dane and Roo, who all go to CCH with me and make up my largest friend group, aka my only friend group. After Jackson stopped talking to me, Evie was the one who took me under her wing and made sure I wasn't lonely, something I'll always be grateful for. Evie is also my polar opposite—tall, loud, and quick to laugh—which is why she promptly drops herself into my lap. All six-foot-two of her. Did I mention she plays volleyball?

"Oof," I say.

"Who's the boy?" She cocks her head at Carlos. "He's cute."

"Carlos, this is Evie Ranier. She lives two doors down from me and likes to monitor my social life."

"That's the truth." Evie slides off my lap into the booth, shoving me over with her hip, then reaches across the table to shake hands with Carlos. "Good to meet you, Carlos whatever." Then, "Hey, I *know* you."

"You do?"

She nods. "Where're you from?"

"New York," he says. "By way of Mexico City."

"Manhattan?"

"Long Island," he admits. "But don't tell anyone. You'll ruin my reputation."

"You're funny," Evie says approvingly. "Hold on, did you

go to camp in the Berkshires with Tabby Fowler? That place that had to change its name?"

Carlos sits back, holds his hands up. "Busted."

"I *knew* it! Tabs is my cousin. Well, first cousin once removed. But I've seen pictures of you. You guys are bad. In a good way, of course. Like, in the *best* way."

I poke Evie in the side. "Why'd the camp change its name?"

"Some kid drowned or something. Or maybe it was lightning." She turns to me. "Did you get a look at Dane and Roo? Something happened last night and now I think they're *flirting*. It's ridiculously cute."

I peer around her but don't see them anymore. It's too crowded all of a sudden. "Maybe they went outside. Wait, who drowned?"

But Evie's moved on. "We missed you last night. Mel and Zandy went in the water and Mel got bit by a seal. He had bite marks on his ankle. He's probably going to need rabies shots."

"Can seals have rabies?" Carlos asks.

"I don't see why not," Evie says. "They're mammals."

"Now I'm trying to picture a rabid whale."

Evie laughs before turning to me: "Hey, so where were you, Miss Mysterious? You never answered my texts. You missed everything."

"I wasn't in a party mood," I say.

"But what were you doing? Hooking up with your secret boyfriend here?"

"Pretty much."

She laughs and kisses me on the cheek and asks if I'm going to be studying later, which I tell her I am and that she should stop by. The whole time, I feel the weight of Carlos's gaze on me, but he says nothing.

"Oh, there's Roo!" Evie points wildly. "I'd better go. Nice meeting you, Summer Camp Carlos. I'll tell Tabs you say hi."

He smiles. "Good meeting you, Evie Ranier."

She hops up and scoots off, and I turn back to Carlos, to try and explain why Evie doesn't know about Jackson yet or how I can just up and lie to a friend's face. But it's too late. He's already out of the booth.

"I think I should go, too," he says, and before I can answer, he's gone.

HOME ABOUT NEWS ARCHIVE

TRUEMAINE.COM

Home Page for the State of Maine . . . and Murder . . .

"Without Justice"

Someone close to me once said that an unsolved murder is like a tumor. It wreaks havoc in the place where it grows, but left unchecked it can also spread, seeding illness into more parts of the body until there's no hope for survival.

I think this is a decent description of how Chrissy Lambert's death was felt across Cabot Cove. The initial search for her killer focused on the usual suspects: a boyfriend, a couple of locals with criminal records, including one who'd previously abused a minor. But none of these leads panned out. The boyfriend had an airtight alibi—he was attending an admitted student event at MIT, which was confirmed by multiple witnesses—and the two ex-cons were both in their eighties and deemed physically incapable of carrying out the crime. In the end, no one was ever charged with her death. Her family was—and still is—devastated.

But those who knew and loved Chrissy weren't the only ones changed by her murder. From what I understand, the whole town changed. Local parents grew fearful and distrusting, first of strangers, then of each other. And in the five years after Chrissy was killed, the following events occurred:

- A group of concerned homeowners from the wealthy Seacrest neighborhood established Cabot Cove's first ever neighborhood Crime Watch chapter. Initially an open group, members met regularly to discuss crime-stopping solutions and general safety concerns, before evolving into a more selective membership organization—the Seacrest Homeowners Association.

- The Sheriff's Office budget was increased by 20 percent after Sheriff Morris Kendall campaigned and won reelection on his promise to hire additional deputies for a newly launched Violent Crime and Drug Enforcement Task Force, in a county with one of the lowest crime rates in the country.
- For the first time in its history, the Cabot Cove Unified School District began charging parents for after-school care services. This change was justified on the basis of needing to pay for upgraded safety measures, including metal detectors, new lighting and alarm systems, and the hiring of two full-time security guards.

What do these changes have in common? Chrissy Lambert's name was used as a rallying cry for all of them, because they were intended to make our community safer.

But have they?

I've been doing a lot of digging lately, and I've discovered something disturbing. In the past eighteen months, *four* Cabot Cove teenagers have gone missing. All of them vanished without a trace, leaving behind wallets, cell phones, and loved ones. Their names are:

Sign up for our newsletter!

Trent Michaels, 17
Iris Mulvaney, 16
Eden Vicente, 15
Benson Horace, 17

Of these four, only one has been found: fifteen-year-old Eden Vicente, who was a freshman at Broadmoor Academy last year. In her case, sheriff's deputies and members of other law enforcement agencies actually sounded the alarm, and Eden's body was eventually recovered from Lake Paloma. This is close to where she went missing, and her death has been ruled an accident. But the three Cabot Cove teens have yet to be located. No one has any idea what might've happened to them.

And now, as of this morning, there's news that another teen may soon be added to the list. Someone who is deeply loved and deserves for his city to move Heaven and Earth to bring him home safely. It's the same effort and care that Trent, Iris, and Benson deserve and have yet to receive.

So here's my question for you, TrueMainers: How can we make people pay attention? How can we make people care when it's the townies—not the boarding school students—who are lost?

Be safe out there,

Yours truly,
—the Downeast Girl

Sign up for our newsletter!

10

SUNDAY MORNING, I WAKE UP to a text from Aaron Kanofsky, one of the co-owners of TrueMaine.

"Call me NOW," it says, and I do.

"What the hell were you thinking?" Aaron snaps, and I'm not used to the anger in his voice. Aaron and his brother Vince developed the site with the intention of "disrupting" crime reporting and crime statistics by "putting the power into the hands of the people," whatever that means. Well, I think it's supposed to mean that TrueMaine reporters follow tips and cases based on upvotes from a given community rather than just covering whatever story the corporate media decides is relevant on a given day. The infotainment business model, they call it. Anyway, when they hired me to write on the unsolved mysteries of Cabot Cove, I was told I could post whatever I wanted. There's no editorial process because my content is just window dressing. Probably for investors, according to Jackson, but so far the agreement works for me.

"Is something wrong?" I venture.

"Yeah, a lot's wrong," he says. "That column you posted last night—"

"You didn't like it?"

"You know, I give you a lot of leeway, Bea, because you post regularly, unlike the majority of our writers, who either flake on us or think they're the next Truman Capote and want us to reimburse them for their 'research,' dear God. But you, your content's usually well sourced and solid—maybe a little heavy on the 'cub reporter' earnestness—but *this*, what you put up, this isn't what we talked about. You're supposed to be writing about cold cases from the past. Ancient history. Not current news and especially not tabloid-style gossip."

"Gossip?"

"We don't give people pitchforks. They can do that on their own."

"Well, I'm sorry," I say, and I hate how whiny my voice sounds, all trembly and weak. "I didn't think of what I was writing as news. It was just how I was feeling."

"But you published your *feelings* on my site. I mean, are any of these facts true? Or are they just rumors?"

"Of course they're true. Everything in the column is factually accurate."

Aaron's voice softens. "So some kid's really gone missing? Who is it? Do you know?"

"His name's Jackson Glanville."

"Hold on." He pauses. "Yeah, okay. That tracks. That's the name that's out there. I guess Vin and I need to talk with legal about how we want to proceed. Honestly, this might be okay if we play it right and push the political angle."

"What political angle?" I ask.

"Look, we'll talk soon. Just don't post anything else until you hear from us. Okay?"

"Sure." My heart's pounding. "Wait, what do you mean the name that's out there? I didn't name anyone in my post."

"Have you checked the comments?"

"No."

He gives a low laugh. "Well, you should. And I don't say that lightly."

Aaron hangs up and I grab my laptop and log on to my TrueMaine account. The site's still new—it only launched nine months ago—and most of the engagement remains in the user forums, not the main content. Supposedly, at the one-year mark, some big relaunch is going to happen where the whole interface will be more interactive, featuring videos, live Q&As, and two podcast series. One'll be focused on the New England Mafia and the other, alarmingly titled "Celebrity Cryptid Faceoff," will highlight D-list celebrities who've had encounters with the supernatural. So it seems a little ridiculous to get wound up about *anything* I've written. Usually I'm lucky if I get a single comment on my posts, and most are of the "I make $2,000 a MONTH working from HOME and so can YOU!" variety.

I scroll down and hold my breath. I mean, I just posted last night, and that was a Saturday. Not exactly prime-time news hours.

I blink. Holy crap. There are *fourteen* comments already. And it's only eight in the morning. Who are these people? And where did they come from? Right then, my phone vibrates beside me. I glance down and see it's my shrink, Dr. Wingate, calling.

On a Sunday morning?

Not now. I can't deal with any probing questions or inquiries into my mental state, so I hit ignore and return my attention to the laptop screen. Scrolling to the very top of the comments, I start to read:

Who's missing? What happened? I haven't seen anything on the news, but I heard sirens today out past the west end, near Betty's place. Those Wallaces keep their drapes drawn at ALL HOURS. You might want to check there.

STOP SPREADING LIES. Our city is safe.

It's not lies. Sex traffickers are sneaking in from Mexico. They've been doing it for years to steal our children and sell them. Our governor lets them. It's called corruption. You can look it up.

Get a map already. No one from Mexico is coming to Maine, you brain worm infested nitwit. I bet you think the Chinese army is invading from the Canadian border too.

It's those vaccines. I warned you all! These kids are dying from whatever gene therapy the govt put into them last year and

they don't want you to know. Prove to me how it's safe to put that poison into our kids' arms. I'll wait. #hoax #fakepandemic

It's Jackson Glanville. That's the missing kid. No one can find him. Everything in this article is true and it's being covered up like always. #findjackson #savethecabotcovefour

Barney's right about the vaccines! When that Broadmoor girl died, her body was full of toxins. They were going to do an autopsy, but her family had her cremated and whisked her back to Kentucky. Follow the $$$$.

Jackson???? No! I don't believe it.

O my god.

He's in my homeroom. He's the nicest guy.

Stop talking about vaccines already! They need to inoculate this town against YOU!!!

Bet you anything he killed himself. Kid was in the psych ward a couple years back. And you know who his grandpa was—the Jack in the Box Bomber. That kind of evil is in the blood.

The mom's the one to watch out for. Her family profits from war and she's just as craven.

Hey, hey there, whoever wrote this, you're doing a good job and getting close to what you're looking for. Keep digging, all right? And remember, a shadow government is not your friend. That's just what they want you to think. The surveilled will never be helped by more surveillance.

I sit back with a sick feeling coiling in my gut. I don't know what I was expecting but this is *a lot*. Also, Aaron's concerns make sense now; most of the comments have been posted through the Facebook interface, so it would appear my column's been shared or linked in some local Cabot Cove group, setting off a chain of what can only be classified as . . . gossip.

I read through it all again. One comment strikes me as uniquely insensitive. Comparing suicide and mental illness with a string of serial bombings? Or suggesting Jackson deserves death because of his grandfather?

The final comment, however, is just plain strange. What *shadow government* is there in Cabot Cove? Fair warning about surveillance, I guess, but that doesn't mean we have to accept apathy. Surely, someone can do *something*. Surely, we should care about one another.

Right?

On impulse, I click on the last commenter's username: *theuncouthswain*. Unsurprisingly, their account is dated today and it's their first and only comment. At least it's not one of the vaccine debaters, who show up to fight on pretty much any article even slightly related to public health and safety. My current theory is that both sides are written by the same person intent on acting out their own personal psychodrama or online performance art.

My phone vibrates again, and I grab for it, expecting to hear Dr. Wingate's soothing voice asking how I am. Instead, it's Evie.

Her voice is breathless, wild. "You're coming tonight, right?"

"What are you talking about??"

"The vigil," she says. "There's a vigil planned for tonight. On the beach. It starts at sundown. We're supposed to bring candles."

I freeze. "A vigil?"

"Oh my god," she says. "Didn't you hear?"

"Hear what?"

"The anonymous blog that was all over Facebook this morning. Everyone's talking about it. Even my mom." Her voice lowers. "I think more's going on than anyone's even saying. Like something big. I can't believe you don't know yet."

"Just tell me," I urge.

"It's Jackson Glanville," she says. "He's *missing*."

11

THE FIRST TIME I EVER went to see a psychiatrist, I was eleven years old, freshly grieving my mother's death, and so knotted with anxiety that I couldn't go to sleep or to school, and I melted into a panicky mess every time my father left for work. My mind was racing so fast, all the time, like a weasel on a wheel, that I was essentially stuck. I couldn't do anything, not even when I entered the psychiatrist's home office and saw it was filled with toys and a sand table and games and even an Xbox connected to a television. Rather than risk touching anything I wasn't supposed to, I just stood awkwardly on the carpeted floor while a slim bearded man with sharp blue eyes and silvery hair introduced himself.

"I'm Dr. Wingate," he said with a smile.

"I'm Beatrice." I watched him closely. Dressed in neat jeans and a plaid button-down shirt, Dr. Wingate didn't look like any doctor I'd ever seen before. More like one of Maine's moose hunting tourists. Or someone with ample access to the employee discount at Bean's.

He gave me a tour of the room and even took me outside into his garden to show me a large koi pond. The fish crowded close as we approached, mouths gaping, their thick orange-and-black scales gleaming in the sunlight. Dr. Wingate handed me a small cup filled with pellets to toss into the water. The fish swirled and splashed as they ate before retreating to cooler depths.

"My father says you live here," I said when we returned to the ground floor office. My dad, in fact, was sitting above us, in a small waiting area on the first floor—the house was built into a hillside—reading a science journal while I had my appointment.

"That's right," Dr. Wingate said. "This is where I work, and upstairs is where I live."

I gestured at the toys. "Do your children get to play with these?"

"No," he said. "My wife and I don't have children."

I remember that surprised me. I'd assumed all husbands and wives had children. Wasn't that the whole point of marriage? But Dr. Wingate went on to explain that being childless meant he could dedicate all his time to his clients. Still, I wondered, what did his wife think? Was it her choice or his? The idea was captivating in a strange way. Here I was, a motherless child, and living in this very home was a woman who would never become anyone's mother.

"Do you know what privacy is, Beatrice?" Dr. Wingate asked, once we'd sat across from each other in matching upholstered chairs.

I nodded. "It's when someone wants to be left alone."

“That’s right!” He beamed at my answer. “Sometimes people want to be alone physically, and sometimes people don’t want to share things about themselves that are inside them. Like thoughts or feelings or things that have happened. Respecting someone’s privacy means allowing them to choose how and when they share personal information—not doing it for them. Does that make sense?”

“Yes,” I said.

“Well, I want you to understand that as a doctor, I am bound by law to keep the information that you tell me in this room private. We call this doctor-patient confidentiality. However, because you are a child, your father has the right to know certain things about you, although I would never share anything with him without telling you first.”

“Okay.”

“Additionally, there are a few other situations in which I might have to break confidentiality in order to keep people safe.”

At the mention of safety, I furrowed my brow in confusion. Did that mean he could keep me from getting sick like my mom had gotten sick? Alas, he’d gone on to explain that if I ever told him about any instances of child abuse or children being harmed, or if I’d harmed myself or threatened another person, he might have to tell the police. Or child and family services. Maybe even the person I was hypothetically threatening. I listened attentively, eager to know the rules. Ultimately, though, the whole thing was a letdown since "breaking confidentiality" turned out to be more akin to tattling than any kind of medical miracle.

"Do you have any questions for me?" he asked.

I considered my response carefully. "What if you think someone's hurt someone else, but you aren't sure? What if you can't prove it?"

His expression stoic, Dr. Wingate leaned forward, softened his voice. "Is this about you? Are you wondering if someone hurt you?"

"No, it's my friend," I said quickly. "And this is something that happened a long time ago."

"Why don't you tell me about it."

"Wouldn't I be breaking my friend's privacy?"

"You're doing it to ensure your friend is safe. Plus," he reminded me, "I don't even know who it is."

That was certainly true. I nodded and continued, "Well, it happened the summer my friend and I visited his grandfather's horse farm." Settling back in the overstuffed armchair, I recounted the time when I was stung by a bee and Jax had had his nose bloodied, his eye bruised.

"Where is your friend's grandfather now?" Dr. Wingate asked.

"He died," I said. "Last year. It turned out he was a serial killer. He sent bombs through the mail."

This raised Dr. Wingate's eyebrows in a way that mirrored Jackson's response whenever I told him something startling or distasteful. "Oh my. Well, what you've described to me *would* be something I would have to report. Hitting his grandson and bloodying his nose is abuse. However, if the grandfather's dead, there's no risk of him doing it again."

"That's not the only time something's happened to him, though."

"With your friend's grandfather?"

"No." I shook my head. "See, this is the part that confuses me. We were at his grandfather's farm and no one else was there. Except, for this one time. The time that's in this dream I have, and so I don't know if it actually happened."

"You think someone else might've hurt your friend? Someone who knew his grandfather?"

"Maybe," I say. "I didn't see it happen. I just know they were there."

"Who?"

"I don't know. A friend? But his grandpa wasn't the type of guy who had friends. He was mean. We had to cook all our own food."

Dr. Wingate scratched at his beard. "I don't know that there's enough information for me to make a report. Especially since it's from a dream. But we could try. We could do it together, if you'd like. We could call Child Welfare. Or . . ."

"Or what?" I asked.

His eyes glittered with sudden intensity. "Have you tried talking with your friend about this? Asking him what happened? What he remembers?"

At this, I'd laughed nervously, recalling Jackson's dark

moods and his parents' cruelty, which I didn't dare speak of in that room or anywhere. Even thinking about it had me sinking my body deeper into the chair as if I were trying to press myself through the upholstery. "No, no way. Absolutely not. I definitely couldn't do *that*."

12

By Sunday evening, my anxiety's out in full force; Jackson remains missing, there's a vigil to attend, and ultimately none of this is about me and I really need to pull myself together. Humbled, I go to my father and ask for a Xanax from the bottle that he keeps locked up for me, and I also ask if he's willing to accompany me. He says yes to both, and we walk to the beach together, carrying glass jars with tea candles inside that flicker and glow in the cool October dusk.

Overhead, the sky darkens, swirling into a maelstrom of twilight and storm clouds. A few spatters of rain fall as we make our way toward the water's edge, punctuating my mood, and I hate this. The fact that Jackson's missing. That there's a vigil. That I was so close to helping him only to have it fall apart.

Everything.

Beside me, Dad remains quiet. He's a thinker and a daydreamer, so I never take his silence personally, but I can also sense his exhaustion. It's in the slump of his shoulders. The droop of his head.

"You okay?" I whisper.

He turns and smiles that warm dimpled smile that's

guided us both through our darkest days. It's the one my mother fell in love with their freshman year at Michigan, and the one that still gets women to flirt with him in the supermarket line. "I'm fine," he says. "I just wish I'd known what was going on with Jackson. You can always come to me, you know. If you or your friends are struggling."

I snort. "Did you go to Gram and Poppy when you were fifteen and your friends were struggling?"

"I wish I had." He pulls up the hood of his jacket as another burst of rain comes through.

I look at him. "Really?"

"Yes, really. There are some problems you're not equipped to handle at that age. Maybe any age. Only it's hard to see that when you're younger because you want so badly to be able to handle it."

"What kind of problems?" I'm aware my father grew up in this town, but my impression of his youth is that it was flawless in that way you see on television. Safe and sterile streets. Middle-class family. Good schools and just enough adventure with the sea at his doorstep and miles of land open for exploring.

But the sigh he gives is a weary one. "There's always darkness lurking under the surface in a town like Cabot Cove. Only it's impolite to talk about and so people go on and on about the weather and how dangerous the cities are and if the Red Sox will finally win the Series this year. They never talk about what matters. Or what's hurting the people right in front of them. There's a kind of evil in that. In refusing to open one's eyes."

Chrissy Lambert comes to mind, only my dad's already told me he doesn't remember her death. He says it's the kind of thing adults would've whispered about over drinks and kept hidden from children. Kind of like what he and Uncle Abe did when Jax's grandfather died.

"Did you know people who were hurting?" I ask him.

"Absolutely. A kid Abe and I worked with one summer ran his motorcycle into a wall after a fight with his girlfriend. That was my senior year. He'd been drinking and we shouldn't have let him drive, but we didn't know how not to."

"That's awful," I say.

"There was another thing that happened the summer after that. It involved some of the Broadmoor kids, but there wasn't much I could personally do, I guess. That was more something Abe got pulled into."

"Wait, what was it?" I ask. "What'd he get pulled into? Was it a game?"

"What's going on over there?" His voice tense, my dad's eyes suddenly widen, and I turn and follow his gaze, squinting into the hazy night. The mist is rolling off the ocean, but we're approaching the beach parking lot, which is lit by streetlamps and crowded with people streaming in for the vigil. But there's also a group of people I don't recognize. They almost look like protesters, standing together in a tight line, all dressed in black, and they're blocking the lot's vehicle entrance while holding up handmade signs and wearing tape over their mouths.

It's not until we get closer that I can read the messages they've brought:

FIND THE CABOT COVE 4

WHERE'S JACKSON?

DEMAND JUSTICE FOR OUR CHILDREN

#TRUSTTRUEMAINE

My legs go weak.

"Who are the Cabot Cove Four?" Dad whispers.

"I don't know what's going on," I manage to say.

"Isn't that the website you're writing for?" My father points to one of the signs. "TrueMaine?"

I nod, surprised he's recognized the name. Of course, I told him about my column, but I doubt he's ever read it. That's not to say he doesn't care or isn't proud of me. It's just that as a single dad and full-time scientist, he has limited time to spend on extracurriculars. Plus there's really only one relative I talk to about my writing—although trust me, her advice is invaluable.

We pass the line of protesters—I still don't recognize any of them—and head for the access trail leading down to the beach. It's steep, and as we step onto the path, my breath catches at the sight below. It's stunning. The ocean shimmers with shadow and moonlight, and standing there, at high tide, on the neat half-moon curl of sand, are what look like *hundreds* of people, all holding jarred candles, flashlights, glow sticks, and more.

For Jackson.

My throat tightens. Bad news travels fast in a town like Cabot Cove. I know this and I also know Jackson is well liked by just about everyone. He's the guy who helps people across the street when the road's icy or who loads your groceries in your car or who offers to shovel their neighbors' driveways. You can't help but notice his goodness and feel warmed by his sincerity. Still, being here is a lot and I don't know what it's all meant to mean. Is this a hopeful moment?

Or the beginning of the end?

I clutch my chest.

"Come." My father nudges me forward and I follow, taking small careful steps through the dirt, trying not to fall.

Upon reaching the beach, we stand in line to pass by a makeshift altar that's appeared in front of the bonfire. People are setting down photos, flowers, note cards, stuffed animals, balloons.

He's not gone, I think fiercely, gripping tight to my candle jar. *We shouldn't be doing this. We shouldn't give up on him. Not yet.*

Not ever.

"Tell me about your work project," I whisper as we shuffle across the beach in the advancing line.

"I don't think you'll find it very interesting," Dad whispers back.

"Please." My voice takes on a plaintive note before it's

snatched up by the wind and thrown to the crashing waves. "I need a distraction."

My father nods, clears his throat. "At the moment, I'm currently the lead developer on a bio-based multitiered monitoring system that my company hopes will assist in the early identification of environmental contagions and outbreaks that have the potential to cause irreversible neurological decline and even death."

Well, that's a mouthful. "Contagions? Like pollution?"

"No. We already have ways of monitoring pollution, thanks to the EPA. Our problem there is enforcement, which the corporations doing the polluting aren't too fond of."

"Okay, yeah. I get it," I say quickly, since the last thing I want is one of his political lectures.

"The contagions we're trying to monitor are rare and naturally occurring, which means they're hard to find until they've already caused damage. Prions are our main target. Although we're also looking at certain fungal species and related enzyme activity."

"What's a prion?" I ask.

"You've heard of mad cow disease, right? Or chronic wasting disease in deer?"

"Yeah."

"Those are diseases caused by prions."

My nose wrinkles. "I thought they were viruses. Or parasites."

"Nope. They're not either of those things—and they're also a little bit of both." My father smiles at my look of confusion. "Prions are amazingly primitive. As a result, they haven't evolved to spread easily, but they're also very difficult to destroy. They're able to survive most common sterilization procedures, like bleach or boiling. Even irradiation. They're pretty close to indestructible. And, by the time our current surveillance tools identify the disease, the source is often difficult to trace and has likely infected others. In fact, there's a possible outbreak cluster going on right now in Canada. Dozens of people with similar symptoms but no known cause. Actually—"

"Why is *she* here?" A shrill female voice rises above the reverent murmur of the crowd and the hiss and roar of waves pounding against the shoreline. "Oh God, Davis, what is she doing here? I won't have this! No way! Not her!"

I'm staring up at my father as he stops talking midsentence, and I watch the expression on his face shift, sliding from droll scientist into paternal defender. He grabs for me, pulling me toward him, while at the same time throwing one arm in front of his body like a shield. I lurch forward, crashing against his chest, as he stumbles back, dragging me through the sand.

"Leave her alone," my father barks. "We just came to show our support."

"Oh, of course you'll protect her. That's what you always do—make excuses for people who aren't worth the time. But do you know what she did, Franklin? Do you know what your little witch did?"

Squirming free from my father's grasp, I whirl around,

shoes filling with sand, and come face-to-face with a stunningly tall woman in a white silk pantsuit, her dark hair whipping in the wind. There's no mistaking who she is. It's Marla Glanville—local socialite, heiress to the Wright family arms fortune, wife to Deacon Glanville, and Jackson Glanville's mother.

I wilt at the sight of her, as she stares me down, daring me to back off, which I would if only I had somewhere to go. Suddenly she lunges for me, teeth bared, her crimson nails long and gleaming. Someone close to us screams and I duck, but not before Mrs. Glanville tears at my neck with her talons. I yelp, shoving her off me. She staggers back amid more screams, white silk coming alarmingly close to the bonfire before she advances again.

My father tries fending her off, tries putting his body between ours.

"Leave her alone, M," he warns.

M? I think and this is when I realize there's blood dripping down my neck, staining the sand beneath me. *How strangely familiar.*

Mrs. Glanville points at me, finger jabbing in the misty night air. "You horrible, horrible child. I know the lies you're spreading about us."

"What lies?" I squeak, and for an instant, I think she's referencing my TrueMaine column. I write under a pseudonym, but maybe she knows somehow. Maybe Jackson told her.

"You went to the *cops*," she hisses. "You told them *we*

were responsible for our dear Jackson's disappearance. How cruel can you be? How hateful!"

My chest swells with resentment. "I never said anything like that!"

"How much suffering am I expected to endure in the face of liars like you?"

"I'm not a liar!" I shout. "I'm not!"

"Oh yes, you are, Bea Fletcher," she says. "You've done nothing but hurt Jackson all these years. And now you want to act like you're saving him? How do I know *you're* not the one responsible for his disappearance? That you haven't gotten him mixed up with something awful?"

"What're you talking about?"

"Someone at the Sheriff's Office said you were the last person to hear from Jackson. That you lured him out of the house and into the woods under false pretenses. What reason would you have to do something like that? Why couldn't you just leave him alone like he wanted you to? Oh God, what have you done with him?"

Her voice cracks on this last word as she falls to her knees and breaks into an unholy wail. The crowd rushes in to support her, to hold her upright. I watch, transfixed, but my father pulls me away, dragging me from this chaotic scene where neither of us are wanted and maybe never were.

This is terrible.

This is all my fault.

"Hurry," my father grunts as we reach the dirt trail we'd walked in on. I nod but glance back one last time to survey the beach, the vigil, this twisted ode to Jackson Glanville. Gatherers not tending to his mother have moved back and are now standing awkwardly on the rocks and sand. Most are watching our departure, but I spot a lone figure perched atop a boulder who has turned away and is gazing out to sea.

Jax, I think madly, but of course it's not him. This figure's too tall. Too old-fashioned in a sleek trench coat and fisherman's cap.

Plus Jax, my Jax, is gone, gone, gone.

Suddenly I place the trench coat and the figure. It's *Dr. Wingate*, I realize with a fresh swell of confusion. What is *he* doing here? Only I don't have time to stop and wonder because my dad tugs harder on my arm and urges me to go, and so the only thing I can imagine is that Dr. Wingate is trying his very, very best not to see me or the mess I've made, and for that, I suppose, I can only be grateful.

13

"You lied to me," Evie says the next morning when I call and ask if she'll get my homework assignments for me. Dad's already left for the office, but he said I could stay home today in light of what had happened at the beach, and I had no problem accepting the offer.

"What?" I'm startled by the vitriol in my friend's voice. I was expecting a little sympathy for that disaster at the vigil last night. For *something*.

"You *knew* he was missing, Bea," she says sternly. "When we saw each other on Saturday, you knew, and even when I called you yesterday you pretended like you had no clue what was going on."

I shake my head, even though she can't see it. "It's not like that. I swear."

"Then what's it like?" she demands.

"It's complicated."

Her voice lowers. "Did you really say those things? About the Glanvilles? That they were responsible?"

"No!" My response comes out louder than I intend. "Of course not."

"But you were the last one to talk to him."

"Maybe."

"This looks weird. You know that right? You reported him missing even before his parents knew he was gone."

I grip the phone. "I reported him missing because he didn't show up at the Hollow Friday night. We had plans. That's all. It wasn't like him, and I was worried."

"How would you know what Jackson was like?"

I'm startled by this question. "What's that supposed to mean?"

"Just that—you two didn't hang out all that much. I know you used to. When you were kids. But not lately. So maybe you don't really know him that well anymore. Not enough to pass judgment on what's normal for him."

"Goodbye, Evie," I say, hanging up, but her words unnerve me. *Of course*, Jax and I hang out. I mean, we didn't for a long time after he was in the hospital. She knows that whole story. It's part of how I became friends with her and Roo and Dane in the first place. But these last six months have been different. Jax was the one who reached out to me to make amends, and he even told me I'd done the right thing back in eighth grade. He'd *thanked* me.

But had I ever told Evie this?

I can't remember.

There's a knock at the front door.

I freeze and drop to the floor, suddenly panicked, which is my anxiety kicking in more than anything, but also who just shows up without calling first? It's not normal. Plus, after last night, I think I'm allowed to be a little jumpy.

After a moment, I build up the courage to crawl to my bedroom window and risk a stealth peek out to see if whoever was at the door has left. My body goes cold. They're still here. *They*, being the operative word; I can see straight down to the front porch, and standing there are two uniformed deputies. Both men.

With a gasp, I duck back out of view and will myself to stay calm. Who are these guys and what are they doing here? Did Lt. Deputy Bernstein send them? My fingers go to my scratched-up neck. I also wouldn't put it past Mrs. Glanville to lodge some sort of complaint against me or a restraining order. I could do the same to her, I guess. Dad had wanted to file an assault report last night when we got home, but I'd talked him out of it.

But what if they're here for other reasons?

Like arresting me?

Okay, that has to be my paranoia talking, but there's another knock on the door and then the doorbell rings so I just lie there on the floor like a dead bug and don't move. Not an inch. At some point, Lemon hops off the bed and walks over to me, brushing her soft head against my cheek, curling her tail.

"Shh," I tell her, then I hold my breath and wait. After what feels like forever, I pop up and peek out the window again. My shoulders sag with relief. The deputies are both gone, and their car isn't visible on the street anymore.

Grabbing the first clothes I can find, I slip into them as quickly as possible. Staying home, lying low, these were good ideas in theory. But now, home isn't safe. Something's going on. Not just with Jax, but with me, and I need to know what it is.

I need to find a way to protect myself.

×××

I'm cautious leaving the house, making sure no one's watching. I tie my hair back and pull my Red Sox hoodie over my head, but once I'm on my bike, I go, pedaling hard and fast, my mind reeling with confusion. What am I not seeing? I go over everything that happened Friday night—calling Jax, making plans to meet. Nothing had seemed off then.

Or did it?

I'd suggested meeting at the Hollow and his response had been *I hate that place*. Followed by: *Those Broadmoor kids make me want to puke*.

But which Broadmoor kids? Jax isn't actually the type to prowl the Hollow on any kind of regular basis, looking for a party, looking for trouble. That place—with its rambling, run-down treehouse—is mostly used for casual hookups and other activities best done in private. And don't get me wrong, there are plenty of people in this town eager for such experiences. But Jax isn't one of them.

As far as I know.

And how well is that?

It's true I hadn't talked to him for almost three years before he'd come back into my life. But that's not to say I didn't see him every day at school, walking the halls, wearing his basketball uniform, taking home nearly every academic award available to our class. Jax was even a tutor for my bio class last year, seeing as he was already taking college-level science classes.

For so long, seeing him around campus, around town, I'd yearned to find the courage to apologize or ask how he was doing, but I assumed I'd just cause him more grief. More than I already had. And selfishly, there was also a sense of relief on my part for no longer carrying the burden of Jax's stresses and sadness. It felt good not to be targeted by his parents' toxic judgment and disapproval. Not to mention, after Jax had returned from whatever program they sent him to, he really did seem better, from what I could tell. More well-adjusted. He'd smiled and laughed. He made new friends and took on new challenges.

And so maybe, I thought, maybe *I* was the problem in his life all along.

I'd shared all this with Dr. Wingate. Lamenting my failures and inadequacies as a friend. To his credit, he'd worked hard to counter these thoughts and taught me skills like positive self-talk and reframing. But wasn't the proof of my guilt evident in my ruined friendship? The one I couldn't bring myself to repair?

Until one day, Jax approached me during school. Asked if we could talk.

It was winter—Maine's most unforgiving season—and we agreed to meet when classes were over in one of the music practice rooms, beneath the main auditorium. Warmed by radiator heat and soundproof insulation, I'd waited there, rehearsing in my head all the ways I'd apologize to Jax, how I'd beg for atonement for what I'd done.

But then the door opened and there he was, fresh from the outside. There was snow on his jacket, snow in his hair, and his cheeks were flushed pink, his blue eyes bright and shining. I'd barely had a chance to register his presence when he'd thrown his arms around me. Held me close.

"Oh, Bea," he'd murmured "I'm so sorry for everything. All these years, I've missed you. I've wanted to tell you that for so long."

"I've missed you, too." I pressed my face against his chest, inhaling his warm scent of soap and sweat. I couldn't believe how tall he was or how strong he'd become. I couldn't believe he was here. With me. "I feel so awful about what I did back then. What I put you through. Please forgive me."

He'd pulled back then, looked me right in the eyes. "There's nothing to forgive, okay? You didn't do anything wrong. I was so confused, and my parents, they convinced me that you'd tried to hurt me. Or humiliate me. Just so you could feel better about yourself. But I know that's not true. It never was. In fact, I owe you all my gratitude. I didn't know how to say it before, but I owe you my life."

"Do you really mean that?" I asked.

"More than you'll ever know," he told me.

× × ×

My legs push hard, carrying me across town where I pick up the local bike path and ride into the Cove's north shore.

It's a brisk day—sunny, clear skies with a cool whip of wind. Unlike the showy south side, homes over here are eclectic and full of personality. Never built to tame nature, houses on the north shore are painted to complement the waves—a smattering of gray, blue, and frothy green, and many have dangling wind chimes, decorative pieces of driftwood and other offerings to the ocean's surging wrath.

Face slick with sweat, I pull up in front of my favorite house—on a corner lot, it's a white Victorian with sharp gables, gingerbread trim, and a white picket fence. Leaving my bike nestled against the porch stoop, I walk up the front stairs and knock softly.

The stout man with thick glasses who answers ushers me in, gives me a tight hug, and kisses the top of my head. "Good to see you, Bea."

"How's she doing?" I ask.

"Not bad. I think the new treatments are helping and she's been up and in the garden a few times. I brought over a pot pie last night. My uncle used to tell me it was her favorite, although I always suspected he meant it was his. But help yourself to leftovers. I'm heading out to the farmers market."

"Thank you, Dr. Hazlitt." I wave goodbye and watch him leave, as a rush of longing comes over me. My greatest wish would be to have such a dedicated group of friends and family all willing to drop by and care for me when that kind of care is needed. Only when I envision my own future, the end of my years, the only thing I can picture is being alone.

None of this is to say that my great-aunt—technically my

great-*grand*-aunt, I guess, but that's a real mouthful—is totally helpless. But two knee replacements and semi-severe spinal degeneration have limited her mobility. Chronic pain from arthritis hasn't helped much either, although a new treatment has been offering her a moderate amount of relief, which is kind of amazing.

I tap my fingers against her bedroom door, worried she might be dozing. Worried she might not have time for me when I so desperately need her wisdom and love.

"Come in, Bea," she says, so I do and the thing about Aunt Jess is that even through her aches and pains, she's as observant as ever, which means she knows something's wrong the instant I step into the room. She holds her arms out and I go to her, the tears falling before I even know they're there.

14

"YOU'RE DOING ALL THE RIGHT things," she says, gently stroking my curls after I've explained what's happened, what I've done, and how terrified I am about it all.

"What if it's my fault?" I whimper. "What if I'm responsible for whatever's happened to Jax? And I don't even know?"

"You can't think like that," she tells me. "What-ifs won't do you any good. If you want to know what happened, then you have to follow the clues. Figure it out for yourself."

"How do I do that?"

"You *know* how. It's okay to feel scared or uncertain. But don't let that get in the way. Trust that you know exactly what to do."

I nod, squeeze her hand, and kiss her cheek before extricating myself from her bed and grabbing a basket of clothes that need folding. This was the exact pep talk I needed—the reminder that solutions only come when you work toward them, not when you give up. Also, it feels good to have tasks to attend to. I always try and come by a few times a week to visit with Aunt Jess but also to do laundry and take care of any other chores that need doing. She has a lot of help, thank goodness, and letting her age in her home has been the greatest gift her books have been able to provide. Obviously, that isn't *why* she writes. She does it because it's her passion, and no one's as good at it as she is.

Aunt Jess is also the reason I love mysteries as much as I do and why I'm unapologetic about my interest in the macabre. But most of all, I admire her independence. Widowed early, Aunt Jess fought to make something of her second act as a single woman in a time when that wasn't expected of her. Or even encouraged. But my grandfather was her nephew and she doted on him like a son. In return, he helped her publish her books, launching a legendary career that won't soon be forgotten.

I'm making her a pot of green tea when I get a text from Carlos.

You okay?

Trying to stay hopeful.

Thanks for checking in.

It means a lot.

I don't think I understand everything, but I know a little about what you're going through. So you know, I get it. How lonely it can be. I'm up for meeting again, if you are. Maybe a place with fewer interruptions?

I'd like that.

How about later this week?

Sounds good. I'll be in touch.

Part of me wants to keep texting, to ask more. Like what he was trying to ask me at the coffee shop and how he might know anything about what I'm going through, but I'm warmed from the interaction and the promise of a second chance. Given the way he left on Saturday, I'd assumed he was back to thinking I was just some actor hired to cosplay a mystery for him and his boarding school friends.

The kettle whistles. I slide my phone away, turn, and pour the tea. Then I carry a tray with the pot and teacup into my great-aunt's room.

"By the way, I've been enjoying your column," she says brightly, placing the book she's reading beside her.

"Really?" I can't help but smile as I set the tray down on her nightstand. Other than Jax, my dad, and Dr. Wingate, Aunt Jess is the only person who knows my online identity. "Did you know Chrissy Lambert?"

Her gaze goes distant. "Not personally, no. I was traveling a lot at the time. Although I certainly remember hearing about her death, and you know, Sonny mentioned it to me once, years after the fact, when he'd fallen ill. He told me that the case wasn't what it looked like."

"Who's Sonny?" I ask.

"Sonny O'Malley. Our old medical examiner. He's gone now. Cancer took him in back in 2000."

It takes me a moment to absorb this information. "Medical examiner . . . as in he did Chrissy's autopsy?"

"It's likely. I don't know that for sure."

"What did he mean that the case wasn't what it looked like?"

"He never told me, and I'm sad to say that for once I was too busy to look into it myself," Aunt Jess says. "But you could, you know. If that's what you're interested in."

"Follow the clues," I say.

She smiles. "That's my girl."

I blow air through my cheeks. I *am* interested, obviously. But with so many other things going on . . .

Something pops into my head. "Hey, Aunt J, you'd be proud of me. I solved a riddle Friday night."

"What was it?"

I tell her about meeting Carlos and the twins and the weird Broadmoor game they were playing. And how I solved their riddle despite all their fancy private school education.

My great-aunt smiles. "Posse comitatus. Well done, my love."

"Thank you."

"What was the game you said they were playing?"

"It's like a scavenger hunt thing. They called it tenace."

"Tennis?" she echoes.

"That's what I thought." I spell it for her. "Do you know about it?"

"Well, tenace is a bridge term." Aunt Jess pronounces the word slightly differently. The way she says it, the last syllable sounds more like *ace* than *is*. "It's a type of leverage."

"Leverage?"

"A strategic advantage," she explains.

"Like blackmail?"

"That would be a different kind of leverage. The forceful kind."

"Does it have to do with aces?"

She smiles. "It has to do with being tenacious. Like having the patience to wait for someone else to walk into your trap."

I'm in awe. "You seriously know everything, don't you?"

"I wouldn't go that far." She blows on her tea.

"Isn't it weird that teenagers would name something after a card game only old people play? No offense."

"None taken," she says, "And you're right. But my guess is that teenagers didn't name it. Or if they did, then they haven't been teenagers for a very long time."

"The students I met thought *I* was part of the game. Why would they think that?"

"The Broadmoor students?" she asks.

I nod. "They assumed I was playing a role just for their benefit. And they didn't believe me when I said I was looking for Jackson."

Aunt Jess cocks her head. "How interesting."

"Which part?"

"All of it. I'd like to hear more about this game. If you learn more, that is. If you see these students again."

"I'll tell you everything I learn. I promise."

"Good girl. Anything else going on?"

"Yes! One more thing."

"What's that?" she asks.

"Have you ever heard of Cabot Cove having a shadow government?"

Aunt Jess laughs. "There's only one group in Cabot Cove I've ever heard of being referred to as such. And not in a flattering way."

"What group is that?" I ask.

"The Seacrest Homeowners Association," she says.

15

Follow the clues. Keep digging.

After leaving my great-aunt's house, I hop back on my bike and head downtown toward an unlikely destination: the county records office. It's located a mere block away from the courthouse and the new Sheriff's Office, which makes riding into this part of Cabot Cove feel a little like walking into a lion's den. Is there a warrant out for my arrest?

Are people actively looking for me?

Not being noticed is the best disguise, although my brown skin means I stick out in coastal Maine more than most. Still, I do my best to seem normal and unhurried, as I lock up my bike amid the midday lunch crowd. It's not just the sheriff's deputies I'm worried about spotting me, but also anyone who was at the vigil last night. Anyone who saw me in the center of that god-awful spectacle.

Fortunately, my presence goes unnoticed, and I hurry up the steps to the office building. The architecture is more than a little bleak; it's essentially a two-story cinderblock rectangle with little to no landscaping surrounding it.

Inside's not much better. The sole color scheme is gray,

but as I approach the front desk, I open my mouth to ask a question, then stop.

"May I help you?" the young woman sitting at the reception desk asks.

"What're those?" I point because atop the woman's neat styled black bob is a headband adorned with fluffy white bunny ears.

She reaches up, then laughs. "Oh! I forgot I had them on. It's for Halloween. We're allowed to dress up all month. But our options are limited. No masks or face paint. Nothing bloody or upsetting. You get the idea."

"Sure," I say, but can't stop staring at the ears.

"Can I help you?" the clerk asks again and this time I'm able to articulate what it is I'm looking for.

"Those records aren't digitized," the young woman explains. "You'd have to search the originals by hand."

"Can I do that?"

"Yes, but you can't take the records out of here."

"Can I make copies?" I ask.

"If you fill out an application, you can submit a request for an official copy." Her voice lowers. "If it's not for something official, just take pictures on your phone and save yourself the hassle. Just don't tell anyone I told you that."

My lips press into a smile. "I won't. Thanks."

"Come on." She stands, waves a hand, and in a surreal haze, I follow the rabbit-eared woman down two chilly flights of stairs into the building's subbasement. We enter a narrow corridor and walk halfway down to a steel door marked Records Room B-3. I hang back and wait as the clerk fiddles with her lanyard key chain.

Once the room is open, we both walk in and the clerk flips on the overhead lights, a humming bank of bright fluorescent rods. I look around and see rows of conference tables ringed by wide banks of floor-to-ceiling filing cabinets. It reminds me of a medical office. There's also a separate server room, blocked off by glass windows and doors, and in it I spy what appears to be an ancient mainframe circa whenever Kubrick filmed *2001: A Space Odyssey.*

"Sorry for the frigid temps," the clerk says. "The server has to stay cold. It's not the most up-to-date technology."

"Does it actually work?" I press my face against the window to get a better look.

"It does. It just looks old." She turns and takes off down the rows, inspecting cabinet labels until she arrives at a specific one and begins to unlock a bank of drawers.

"How's everything organized?" I ask, trailing behind her. "By medical examiner? Or the deceased?"

"By date," she answers. "Just to make it a little more fun and remove logic from the process. But here's the general time frame you're looking at. The files you want are probably going to be in this six-month range. If we need to expand that time frame, we can."

I glance at the cabinet and the open drawers. "I can just look through these?"

She nods. "Any files you remove, place them on a table for reading and then leave them there when you're done. We'll put them back. There's a whole system, so please, let us do that."

I agree and thank her, and once the clerk's gone, I reference my notes, then immediately begin pulling files out, setting them on the table closest to me in an effort to chase down the only clue I've been given—Chrissy Lambert's death certificate.

×××

I turn to the files and start selecting the ones I'm interested in. Chrissy Lambert was killed in May 1985, and as suggested, I remove the subsequent six months. With some understanding of the pace at which bureaucracy tends to move—it took two years to get the IRS to stop trying to audit my dead mother, for example—I start from the back, with October 1985.

Multiple papercuts later, my mood's turned grim, reading report after report outlining an individual's death and the circumstances behind it. But then I spot Chrissy's file in the July drawer. My head spins a little when I find it. I feel close to her for reasons not justified by our experiences. She was a wealthy white girl with a politician father who was doted on and loved by all who knew her. I'm none of these things, yet I can't help but be drawn to the horror of her life ending in the way that it did. At the hands of someone who could harbor such hate for her vitality and bloom. In a way, her story reminds me of *The Collector*, that old book where some boring dude wins the lottery, kidnaps a girl, and keeps her in his house. His section of the story is full of petty grievances and self-loathing and reflects a personality so dull and insular and smothering you can't help but feel repulsed. But *her* sections. The girl he's stolen is so vibrant on the page. "I love making," she'd scribbled in her diary, "I love doing. I love being to the full, I love everything which is not sitting and watching and copying and dead at heart."

Returning to the conference table with the file, I pore over the pages, absorbing what I can. Because Chrissy's case was treated as a homicide, an official inquiry was submitted to the Sheriff's Office and the whole thing became part of the public record. As such, the medical examiner's investigation contains witness statements, background information about the layout of the country club, the details of her father's birthday party, as well as where Chrissy was that night and who saw her last.

I read it all with a growing sense of frustration. These details are familiar to me, a rehashing of the same story I've already read about in news reports and seen reenacted on the few crime shows that have covered Chrissy's death over the years. There's nothing new here at all. Maybe Aunt Jess got the case wrong.

Then I notice something. The official report was signed off on by a Dr. Alton B. Vogel. But all the other autopsies I've looked at so far today were performed and conducted by my great-aunt's friend, Dr. Sampson O'Malley, the elected county medical examiner.

I ring the buzzer for the clerk and ask her about this.

She bustles into the room, rabbit ears bobbing, and glances over the report. "Family must've had a private autopsy done. It's not that unusual. Sometimes it's for privacy reasons. But in a high-profile murder case, the family might've done it if they had some reason to believe the local authorities weren't competent or on their side."

"The girl's father was the *mayor*."

She steps back. "Then that is strange."

"Right?"

"Maybe the regular guy was on vacation or something?"

"Maybe." I thank her for her thoughts, although the vacation theory seems unlikely since there are other filed autopsies performed by Dr. O'Malley that are dated from the same time period as Chrissy Lambert's.

I return to the files. After more searching and more papercuts, I find something odd. In the May drawer, filed only two weeks after Chrissy's death, is a document labeled "preliminary death report." Only this one *is* signed by Dr. O'Malley. No mention of Dr. Vogel. It's weird, though, that this document wasn't in the final report. This appears to be the standard protocol—including all earlier findings to document the evolution of an investigation.

But this report wasn't added to Chrissy's file.

Why not?

I start reading and five minutes later, the answer's clear. The thin paper flutters in my hand, as I pore through the document again, ensuring that I understand what I'm reading. Because the events described in these pages are completely different than the narrative I know. The one everybody knows. In fact, it turns my understanding of Chrissy's death—how it happened and who was responsible—completely upside down.

An excerpt of Dr. O'Malley's report reads:

> On the morning of MAY 23, 1985, at approximately 6:42 a.m., an emergency call came through COVE COUNTY EMERGENCY SERVICES requesting medical assistance for a female, later identified as seventeen-year-old CHRISTINE MARIE LAMBERT. Caller reported that MS. LAMBERT had been found unresponsive on the golf course of the Ocean View Country Club. Paramedics arrived at 7:05 a.m. and attempted to administer aid. However, MS. LAMBERT was pronounced dead at the scene.
>
> A subsequent examination of the deceased identified a marked U-shaped furrow [see photo A] running across the front of the throat and noted the absence of traumatic injury to the back of the neck [photo B]. Also observed were the lack of self-defense wounds indicating the deceased had attempted to fight off an attacker. Finally, there were no signs of hemorrhaging or postmortem damage, which would be consistent with manual strangulation.
>
> Preliminary autopsy results conclude that

the probable cause of death is hanging. The width of the deceased's throat wound and initial fiber analysis are consistent with the silk sash from MS. LAMBERT's dress, which was recovered at the scene. Additionally, a lack of physical evidence and overall condition of the body suggests that she was moved onto the golf course after succumbing to her injuries.

Time of death is estimated to have occurred between 7 p.m. and 10 p.m. the night prior, while MS. LAMBERT was attending an event at the Ocean View Country Club. An employee at this event reports seeing MS. LAMBERT enter the ladies restroom at approximately 8:30 p.m. and a subsequent crowd gathering in that space. This is the last confirmed sighting of the deceased, and the employee has also provided this office with what appears to be a note left by the deceased [see attached document] that was later found on the restroom floor. Although the circumstance under which her body was moved currently remains unknown, the note's contents, along with an additional witness report as to MS. LAMBERT's recent despondent state of mind, are all consistent with self-inflicted injury.

A *suicide.* Chrissy Lambert's death was a suicide. She wasn't strangled by any mysterious killer, the way we'd been led to believe. She'd died at her father's birthday celebration, surrounded by party guests and family members who all must've known what really happened. My hands are trembling as I flip to the next page, and there it is. The note she left behind. Written in silver ink on a thick scarlet red piece of stationery, her words read:

Dearest Daddy,

Know that I know you ran A. off for the most pitiful of reasons.

Know that my BA years with him were the very best of my life.

Know that to me, money means nothing.

Know that without him, I have nothing.

Know that without free will, I am nothing.

Nevermore,

C. L.

16

I SIT BACK, STUNNED. THE answer is so obvious and also so damn sad that I don't know what to do with myself. I like to pride myself on my ability to look at a murder case with a different eye. To question the status quo and all the assumptions that come with it. But I never considered *this*. A suicide. A mass cover-up. A daughter's choices denied by her father in both life and death.

Closing my eyes, I picture the blond, bold girl I'd seen in photographs. On her horse. With her friends. I'd assumed her life was as carefree and buoyant as the images she'd let the world see. But she'd lived in Seacrest, same as Jackson, and haven't I always known that appearances can be deceiving?

That people are good at hiding what they can't bear to let you see.

Still shaky, I do what I came to do and pull my phone out to snap photos of all the corroborating documents, all the evidence. When I'm done, I arrange everything neatly on the table as instructed, before leaving the records room and thanking the clerk for her time.

I walk outside in an odd haze of detachment. It's a strange feeling, having an answer and knowing the final *whys* and *hows* of such a sordid and terrible mystery. No one bothers to look at me as I walk down the stairs to the sidewalk, but I bury my head in my phone's glowing screen just in case. Also, I want to check the comments on my last column again.

My stomach knots when I see that a lot of the more recent discussion has to do with *me*. Once again, I'm endlessly grateful Aaron insisted I write anonymously.

Look. The answers are right in front of us. Check the parents. You saw what happened last night. The parents are always the ones responsible. And the parents before them, if you know what I mean.

Bullshit. That girl at the beach is the one who came forward to the cops with her outlandish story about meeting up with him at the Hollow. She's the one they should be looking at. Remember that case out in California with the little girl who vanished and the neighbor who went to the cops? Females can be killers, too, and I wouldn't put it past this one. Sickening.

A little girl in California? This sounds familiar, and a few seconds of fast-fingered internet sleuthing pulls up the relevant information: Over a decade ago, in Tracy, California, six-year-old Sandra Cantu went missing. At a vigil for the girl, a female neighbor, who'd previously reported a suitcase stolen from her home, approached the cops and revealed that she'd found a note on the ground with a handwritten message: "Cantu locked in stolin suitcase." This was all very mysterious, until tragically, the poor girl's body was indeed found stuffed inside the neighbor's missing suitcase, which was located at the bottom of a drainage pond. Confronted with this discovery, the neighbor promptly confessed to the killing.

Evie's "isn't it weird you went to the cops first?" line of questioning reverberates through my head. It *does* seem suspicious, doesn't it? Like, it's exactly what someone would do if they wanted to be seen as innocent.

Swallowing hard, I scroll back to the comments on my column. One more's been added, just since I've been standing here. It reads:

> **The hungry sheep look up and are not fed. 44.398486, -68.532134.**

Huh. That's weird. The sheep part sounds biblical, although I notice that the message was written by the same person who'd commented earlier about shadow governments and who'd urged me to dig deeper into Chrissy Lambert's death: *theuncouthswain*. I engage in more online sleuthing and uncover that both the phrase "the uncouth swain," and the hungry sheep quote are taken from the same Milton poem—*Lycidas*—which is one I'm not familiar with.

Sitting my butt down on the edge of the stone fountain in the cobblestone square outside the courthouse, I pull up the text of the poem on my phone and read through it, the whole thing. First off, it's long. It's also not my taste. Full of flowery prose and invocations of nature, what I glean is that it's about a young shepherd—the uncouth swain—who's been grieving over the drowning death of a childhood friend, Lycidas. There's more to it than that, including an interjected rant about corruption in the Catholic church, but by the end, our narrator states that he's found peace in the knowledge that his friend has escaped all earthly pain and ascended to heaven. That's nice enough, I guess, but not really what I'd call a profound insight.

But why would someone leave this message on my column? Is Lycidas meant to be Jackson? Or maybe Chrissy Lambert? Am *I* the uncouth swain? None of this makes sense. Plus, the quoted line about hungry sheep has nothing to do with the lost friend or accepting the finality of death. It's part of the rant about how the church has failed its flock. Then there are the random numbers at the end of the comment. I'd assumed they were connected to lines or stanzas in the poem, but that doesn't appear to be the case. Also, why would there be a negative value?

A spark of realization hits me. Of course. These numbers aren't a mystery; they're a *place*. I've been on enough of my father's camping trips and hiking expeditions to know what geographical coordinates look like.

Opening the maps app on my phone, I type in the pair of numbers, separated by a comma, and hit enter.

The results come up. For a moment, I stare at the screen,

unsure of how to react. The geographical coordinates left by *theuncouthswain* mark a spot not far from here, and it's a location with connections to both Milton and Jackson. Maybe others, too. Because it's a church, the one where Deacon Glanville serves.

St. John the Baptist.

× × ×

I go despite my better angels warning me away, telling me to avoid Jackson's father at all costs. I go because fear won't be the reason that I don't find my friend. I go because it's all I can do.

Follow the clues.

One thing to know: St. John the Baptist is an Episcopal church, not a Catholic one, and to be honest I don't really know the difference other than the fact that Deacon Glanville was able to join the clergy even when he was married, which feels a little healthier than the Catholic way of letting old dudes who don't have sex decide what's moral and what's not. Or it *would* feel healthier if Deacon Glanville weren't such a monster.

Anyway, it's less than a five-minute ride from downtown, and the church is nestled in the first rise of foothills, perched on a large well-landscaped lot dotted with meeting halls, a playground, and a view down to the water. The sanctuary is located within the main church building—a towering heap of slate and stained glass, built to last the ages. Also contained within these walls is the church's crown jewel: the belfry.

Home to twelve separate handcrafted bells, each

controlled by a complicated wheel-and-pulley system, St. John the Baptist's belfry hosts the sole competitive change ringing group in the entire state of Maine. Jackson's trained with them in the past, and it's fascinating—part sport, part art form. Change ringing groups work in literal harmony, standing crowded together in the narrow bell tower and pulling their individual ropes in calculated intervals to produce the proper rings.

All the bells sit silent now, tucked tight into the rafters. But as I stare up at the belfry from the sidewalk, I spot something moving. Just for an instant—a bright flutter of red. Hand over my eyes to block the glare, I strain to see more, but it's hard to make out what it could be from this distance. The tower windows are frosted and narrow, but sunlight's shining in, and there it is again!

The same flutter of red.

It's likely just a reflection or trick of the light. But the longer I stare, the more I'm convinced that I do see *something*. Or possibly someone. There's the outline of shoulders. A chest—

Oh God.

I start to run as images of Chrissy Lambert's last moments fill my mind. The girl whose own father betrayed her. Had run off her true love for his own selfish reasons and left her bereft.

The church door is heavy. My hand slips, but I grab the iron handle again and pull hard, slipping inside with a sob of frustration. I race up the staircase leading to the second floor, my shoes pounding on carpet, but I make it, gasping, panting, my pulse pounding in my ears. The main corridor is blessedly empty. Bolting forward, I rack my brain to recall which door leads to the belfry. I find it—third door on the left—only there's a sign posted indicating the bell tower's not in service for the next six weeks due to planned maintenance on the bell system.

I push open the door anyway and bound up the narrow metal steps that wind around and around, leading up through the bell tower. My clattery steps echo wildly as my head sways with dizziness, but I hear another sound, too. What sounds like voices, a whole group of them, maybe chanting or somehow in prayer. Gripping the railing, I try peering upward, to see what's visible ahead, but it's too difficult to keep my balance.

When I reach the belfry, it's freezing. At the top of the stairs, I'm hit with a rush of frigid air, and it takes a moment to realize this is because all the windows on the tower's north side have been removed and replaced with temporary plastic sheeting. At this height, the wind blows hard, gusting through the sheeting and filling the space with a wild snap and roar. The bells are shifting gently in their wooden cradles, causing their long ropes to brush against the floor. This is also the source of the sound I heard—less like voices now and more like a siren's song. The whole effect is both terrifying and hypnotic. Not unlike my dream with the creak and groan of that gently swaying barn.

With a shiver, I force myself to walk forward. I don't

know what I expect to find. The worst, I guess, which would be Jackson hanging from the rafters in his red North Face jacket, swinging with the wind like his beloved church bells. A whimper wells in my throat, but then I breathe a long sigh of relief. It's not Jackson at all; there's a red silk flag hung across the eastern window. This is what I saw from the street, and I watch now as the wind catches it, sends the flag fluttering.

But what is it doing there?

What am *I* doing here?

Something scuttles behind me. I whirl around in time to see a shadow dive behind another pile of tarps and a work bench, before making a furtive rush for the staircase.

"Hey!" I call out, lunging forward and pulling back the plastic sheeting. And there, huddled on the floor is a slim figure in jeans and a trucker hat. The person startles at the sight of me, curled in shadow, then suddenly sits up.

"Bea?" they say tentatively. "Is that you?"

17

THE FIGURE STANDS, BACKLIT BY the sun streaming in through the belfry window. They pull off the hat, give a shake of their head, and I watch as a thick swath of dark blond hair tumbles past their shoulders.

"Leisl?"

The girl grins. "The one and only."

"What're you doing?" I ask, and in the daylight, out of the woods, I'm a little stunned by her beauty. I don't know anyone who looks like Leisl, all statuesque and goddess-like and perfect. Or maybe it's more accurate to say people who look like Leisl don't generally know people who look like me—persistently disheveled, slouchy, and with a penchant for resting bitch face.

"What're *you* doing?" she replies tartly.

My mind spins. "This is all very confusing."

Leisl turns and walks to the eastern window. She's wearing a blue gingham crop top and white high-waisted jeans, two items I could never pull off.

"It's not confusing," she calls to me. "It's *perfect*. This is absolutely perfect."

I watch as she reaches to unhook the red flag from where

it flutters in the wind, then gestures for me to take hold of it, too. I rush to help, and together we fold it in the same way I was taught to fold the American flag—corner to corner, followed by a series of diagonal folds that bundles it up tight. When we're done, Leisl slips it into her leather side bag, which she then clasps shut. Something about her movements reminds me of how people describe California—laid-back and carefree and wholly uninclined toward urgency. But of course, she *does* care. She has to. Or she wouldn't be doing this.

"You first." Leisl settles herself cross-legged onto the dusty floor planks across from the open window. Around us, autumn air loops and swirls, ripe with sweet undertones and a deep peaty scent. "Tell me how you got here. All of it. Don't leave anything out."

I sit beside her, back flat against the wall. "It's pretty simple. I'm here because someone left me an online comment containing geographical coordinates that led me to this church."

Her nose wrinkles. "Online comment? Like a DM?"

"No, it was on a true crime site. In the comments section of an article that referenced my friend Jackson. He's the reason I came."

Liesl's laugh rings out, loud and bright, like one of the massive bronze bells currently hanging over our heads. "Are you *serious*?"

"Of course I'm serious. Why wouldn't I be?"

She straightens her spine with a catlike wiggle, tucks hair behind her ears, then clears her throat. "Let me get this straight—in your mind, following a pair of geographical coordinates that you happened to find in the comments section of an article posted on a random internet crime site is a process you would refer to as 'pretty simple'?"

"Well, what would you call it?" I ask.

"First off, how did you know the comment was for you?"

"Oh." I blush. "That's easy. I wrote the article the comment was left on. I kind of have a regular column on the site. It's this Maine-based crime-themed start-up thing. But I use a pen name, so it's not like the comment was for me personally. It was for me—the author of that article."

"So you *do* solve mysteries." Leisl snaps her fingers. "I knew it."

"Not exactly. I present facts. And then sort of crowdsource solutions."

"Like a GoFundMe for justice?" she says.

"Sort of." I don't have the energy to explain it in more detail. "Now tell me how you got here."

"Wait, what's a Maine-based crime-themed start-up?" she asks.

"Just what it sounds like."

"It sounds like an ice-cream flavor." Leisl puts a finger over her lips. "Okay, well, *my* story's not half as interesting as yours. Basically, I was just trying to solve the next part of the clue you helped us with."

"How?"

"It's the church," she says. "The name was in the riddle. St. John the Baptist. Leif told me that was too obvious, but what does he know?"

I blink. "Yeah, you could be right."

"I *am* right, silly. The flag's here. That's the proof. It means the next clue's here, too."

"The flag tells you that?"

"Obviously."

It's not obvious to me, but I glance around the room. "Where is it then? I don't see any clues."

"I don't know," she admits. "But it has to be somewhere."

I look at her. "Well, if you're wondering what I've been up to, I just spent the last couple hours solving an old cold case from the eighties. A girl everyone thought was murdered."

Leisl lifts a brow. "I'm listening."

"It turned out she killed herself. But, sorry, that doesn't have anything to do with what you're looking into."

"You sure about that?"

I wrack my brain, looking for any hint of connection. "You know, one weird thing *did* happen. It doesn't have to do with the girl, though."

"Okay . . ."

"I was at the county records office before I came here. And the clerk there, she was wearing these fuzzy white bunny ears."

"Bunny ears?" Leisl looks doubtful.

"Like a white rabbit! You know, *Alice in Wonderland*. *The Matrix*. That could be a clue, right?"

"Sounds more like a coincidence. Or a costume."

"Maybe," I say. "But your first clue was the posse comitatus, right? And that riddle referenced a shooting in St. John the Baptist Parish in Louisiana, which led you here. And then I got here because I read a comment online, which, in addition to having the church coordinates, included a line from a poem: 'The hungry sheep look up and are not fed.'"

"What does that have to do with rabbits?"

"Hold on." I force myself to slow down. "It'll make sense. I promise. So whoever left the hungry sheep quote, that person had also posted an earlier comment on the same article in which they referenced a 'shadow government' operating in Cabot Cove. They mentioned something about a surveillance state and the dangers of being surveilled."

Leisl perks up at this. "Are you talking about those doorbell cameras? They're evil."

"Evil?"

She lowers her voice. "*They're* the surveillance state. All smart home devices are. They trick people into paying to give up their privacy."

"I think we're getting off topic."

"Don't get me started on ancestry tests," she adds. "It's genetic blackmail."

"Moving on . . ." I say. "My point is that our clues *are* connected. Because in addition to doorbell cameras and ancestry tests, there are others who are watching every little thing that happens in Cabot Cove. I just hadn't put it together with the posse comitatus thing until now. But it makes sense. They're not a literal militia, but they *are* lawless."

"Who?"

"A local homeowner's association. A very powerful one. The Seacrest HOA."

× × ×

Leisl's reaction is a letdown. "An *HOA*? You mean those busybodies that yell at people for not mowing their lawn or leaving their Christmas lights up in January? That doesn't sound very sinister."

"But they *are*," I insist. "The Seacrest group is notorious for how much power they wield and how self-serving they are. They're not interested in stuff like Christmas lights. They act like they're better than everyone and they want to control this whole town. I swear, it's the closest thing to a real live posse comitatus that we have around here. Only rather than militia men, it's a bunch of white women with blowouts."

"Examples, please. Of what they've done."

"Sure." I rub my hands together. "Okay, first off, Seacrest is the oldest and wealthiest section of Cabot Cove. It's gated and you have to pay to drive through it, thanks to their HOA. Anyone who wants to live there has to have approval of the board in order to purchase a home—no short-term rentals allowed. And the board is a nightmare. It's like, all the girls you hate in high school grew up and started an exclusive club that they won't let you join. Although I bet anyone would let *you* join."

"You'd be surprised," Leisl says lightly. "My brother's reputation precedes me."

"Well, in recent years the HOA got the town to put up video cameras to record every license plate that comes into their neighborhood, even though it's illegal per our state's constitution. Their argument is that someone would have to sue to get the cameras taken down and that the city has more than enough money to tie up the case in court for years and no one would bother to challenge it. So far, they've been right. They also hire and pay for their own security guards who respond to any neighborhood complaints well before the sheriff's deputies can get there. Oh, and did I mention they can carry guns? You might think this is meant to keep them safe, but it's also a way to shield their own from actual law enforcement, who they look down on. Can't have an unsightly domestic incident end up in the paper if there's no record of said incident. And obviously there's no recourse for their kids if their parents are abusing them." I pause. "You know, Jackson once told me he thought the private security guards were spying on him. That they were how his parents knew when he snuck out."

Leisl is silent for a moment. "Your friend, was he being abused?"

I nod, shrug, blink back a threatening flood of tears. "Yeah. In a way."

"I'm sorry. I had no idea it was that serious."

"Carlos didn't tell you anything?"

"What about Carlos?"

"Nothing, really." I swipe at my eyes. "He, uh, just texted earlier, to check in, and he asked about Jackson and how I was doing. It was nice."

Leisl snorts. "That's one way of putting it."

"What else would it be?"

"Strategic," she says.

"You're saying he's still playing the game?"

"We're all playing the game."

"Ah."

"Sorry, sorry." She reaches to hug me, just a quick embrace. "That came out meaner than I intended. I like Carlos a lot and you should, too. It's just, well, *I'm* honest about my intentions. That's all. I'm playing the game, but I also really like you. Those are two separate facts. And I *am* genuinely sorry about Jackson."

"Thank you," I say.

"Can I help with anything?"

"Maybe. I've been doing some research and it turns out Jackson's not the only person to disappear in Cabot Cove recently. Four other teens have, too. Including one from Broadmoor, but she was eventually found dead. Eden Vicente."

"Oh." Liesl nods knowingly. "So *that's* why you mentioned Carlos."

"What do you mean?" I ask.

"Well, Eden—she was his girlfriend."

18

MY HEAD CLOUDS WITH CONFUSION. "His *girlfriend*?"

Leisl's voice grows hushed. "It was awful, what happened. Eden was *super* sweet. Quiet, though. I was kind of mad at first, getting paired with a frosh during my sophomore year, but whatever. She always seemed mature for her age. At least compared to the other brats in her grade, who I can't stand. They're all into custom scents these days and walk around smelling like my grandmother's underwear drawer. It's vile. Anyway, Eden played flute. Loved bird-watching and horses. She grew up on a farm in Kentucky. Super wholesome. She and Carlos only went out for a few months. Mostly they made moony eyes at each other, and she'd play flute for him in the meadow, which . . . barf. Anyway, Leif and I really got to know Carlos during the whole search for her. He was distraught."

"I was there," I say. "When she was missing. I volunteered with the search party."

"Really?" Leisl rests her head on my shoulder, like it's just something she's comfortable doing with any old person. "That's so funny. Maybe we've already met."

"It's possible."

"That was a bad time. It was really sad."

"Do you know anything about what happened to her? Other than what was reported?"

"Probably not anything you don't. Just that she went on a hike with the school's outdoor adventure club one weekend. She really liked being outside. I did know that. They headed out to some spot where there's a lake?"

I nod. "Lake Paloma. It's in the mountains. Probably a four-mile hike from your school. It's beautiful."

"Well, everyone who was there that day agreed Eden must've gotten separated from the group on the way back. But no one noticed she was gone until they'd returned to campus. Or if someone did notice, they didn't say anything. I always thought that was suspicious. Kind of like that dive boat that left those people behind in the ocean. Who doesn't count? Anyway, you know the rest—a week later, a diver finds her in the lake. Only she didn't drown."

"What do you mean?"

Leisl lowers her voice. "This is just a rumor, but I heard when they did the autopsy that her lungs were filled with salt water."

"So she *did* drown."

"The lake is freshwater."

I lean back. "You actually saw these autopsy results?"

Leisl shudders then sticks her tongue out. "Uck. No. I hate stuff like that. Thinking about dead bodies or what's in them."

"We must be opposites. I just spent the day reading old medical examiner reports."

"About *Eden*?" she asks.

"No, it was that unsolved murder case from the eighties. Or not murder, as it turned out. But legally, you can't access death records that are less than ten years old so we couldn't get Eden's even if we wanted to."

Leisl sits up. "Tell me more about the eighties girl."

"Chrissy Lambert. That's her name. And like I said, it turns out she hanged herself at this fancy party. But her father was the mayor, and apparently, he staged her body out on the golf course and had some private examiner come in and do an autopsy that ruled her death a homicide. The original one was mislabeled and buried in an old filing cabinet. Until today."

"Why would her father do that? You think he was embarrassed or something?"

"I think he felt guilty about running off his daughter's boyfriend. Or paying him off. Or maybe he just felt entitled to rewrite history to suit the truth he wanted. It must have taken a lot of coordination to pull off burying the first autopsy and keeping all the party guests quiet all these years. Unless . . ."

"Unless what?"

"Unless the people who were at the party felt guilty, too, for some reason. Maybe they'd pressured Chrissy. Or hurt her in some way. You want to see the note she left?"

Leisl nods and I pull up the photo I took on my phone. She reads it and her eyes go wide. "Her boyfriend was from *Broadmoor*?"

"Where'd you get that?" I ask.

She points at the screen. "'BA' is where they spent the best years of her life. Broadmoor Academy."

"Interesting." Why hadn't I put that together? "Is there a way to figure out who this guy is? Or was?"

"Why?" she asks. "Kind of sounds like a waste of time. You already know what happened."

"He could know something we don't."

"Something that ties back to your missing friend?"

"Maybe. I don't know exactly."

"Fine." Leisl rereads the note. "Let's see. Well, you're right that it sounds like the dad bought him off, so he couldn't have been rich. Maybe he was on a scholarship?"

I nod. "There was mention of him possibly going to MIT. So he must've been really smart."

"Okay, so then maybe Daddy agreed to pay his tuition there and he dumped her." Leisl shrugs. "Kind of douchey on the boyfriend's part, but I can see his point. It's MIT logic. He's leaving Cabot Cove anyway. Why not take the money when he goes?"

I scowl because I don't see the logic in hurting another person. "Were there a lot of scholarship kids at Broadmoor in the eighties?"

"Don't know," she says. "I can try and find out. Meanwhile, do you think you could not mention any of this to Carlos? Or my brother?"

"But I thought you were a team. The three of you."

"Bad faith, remember?" Leisl hesitates. "Let's just say

the boys don't always take my ideas seriously. I kind of want to prove them wrong."

"I won't tell them anything," I promise. "But hold up. Are you admitting that looking into this guy *isn't* a waste of time? After you grilled me about it? It feels like there's something you're not telling me."

"So perceptive," she says slyly. "And yeah, it took me a moment to register, but he's *definitely* worth looking into. Everything about this story is."

"Register what?"

She points to my phone. "*That's* the clue we've been looking for."

"Chrissy Lambert's suicide note? How can you know that?"

"What color is the paper she wrote it on?"

I look back at the screen, even though I already know the answer. "It's red."

Leisl makes a whistling sound and starts circling the air with her index finger. "Time to grab your tinfoil bunny ears, girl. 'Cause we're heading down the rabbit hole . . ."

"I'm so confused." I rub my temples. "I hope you know that I don't understand anything that's going on right now."

She laughs. "Yeah, that's kind of what it's like at first."

"What's like?" I ask.

"Playing the game."

×××

It's getting late.

We both agree we need to go, and somehow, we're able to sneak from the church, sight unseen, and slip back onto the streets of Cabot Cove in the dwindling afternoon light. Outside, the air's got some real bite to it—more winter than ocean breeze—and I watch as goosebumps rise on Leisl's bare arms.

I hold my bike's handlebars as we say our goodbyes, promising to update each other on what we find out about scholarship students, sinister homeowners associations, and hungry sheep. We also reiterate our vow to keep this meeting secret, and as we part, I can't help but wonder if *this* is why the game exists. Not to find secrets but to make them.

To generate a sense of wonder in this world.

I'm halfway home when I feel my phone buzzing in my pocket. I stop to see who it is, holding my breath with one foot balanced on the curb as cars whiz by.

It's my father.

"Where are you?" he barks.

"With a friend," I say.

"You said you were staying home."

"From *school*."

His sigh's an exasperated one. "Well, you need to come back here. Now."

"Why?" I ask.

"Two deputies from the Sheriff's Office are here. They want to talk to you."

19

AS A RULE, MY FATHER is not a scary person. He's slow to anger and doesn't hold grudges. I don't even think he's *capable* of holding a grudge, which is a quality I admire but definitely don't understand.

Still, fifteen minutes after his phone call, I'm seated on the worn tweed couch in our living room, he's in the armchair, and two uniformed sheriff's deputies are standing in the center of the room, staring at us both. No air of familiarity or small-town cop charm wafts off this pair, and even from a distance, I can read my father's body language—the tight jaw and folded arms. The throbbing vein over his left brow.

He's *pissed.*

Part of this must be due to him being called home from the office on account of deputies wanting to talk to his kid. That's not a good look, and I already know how important this new project is to him. But whether his rage is misdirected or not, I am internally applauding the fact that he's currently harnessing it all at Marla Glanville.

"You should know that that woman physically assaulted

my daughter last night," he spits, reaching to pull at his necktie before slamming a fist on the arm of the couch.

"Who?" The older of the two deputies—Deputy Shin—takes a step forward, and the expression on his slightly heavy, slightly weatherworn face is seemingly one of concern and empathy. The other guy, I don't know about. His name's Deputy Williams, and he's a lot younger, a lot less serious. Physically, he's short, with a baby face and a thick bristly sex pest mustache, leaving the impression he didn't have a lot of employment opportunities other than ones where he might be allowed to carry a gun. I watch, unsettled, as a faint smirk rises to his lips at the mention of someone assaulting me.

"Marla Glanville," Dad snarls through clenched teeth. "Last night she attacked my Beatrice—unprovoked—and scratched her neck until it bled."

"I wasn't aware of this," Deputy Shin says.

"Show them."

"Dad . . ." I say meekly.

"Do it," he insists, so I lift my chin, pull down the collar of my sweater, and find the light. The older cop leans in, nods. Writes something down.

"She really did that to you?" he asks me.

"Yes."

"You hurt anywhere else?"

I shake my head, and he steps back, goes into lecture mode. "You're welcome to file an official report, if you'd like. I'd personally recommend it just to have it on the record, but the choice is up to you. In my experience, dealing with people like the Glanvilles can be . . . unpleasant. I would, however, recommend having a doctor look at that wound. We can document it, but a medical record is always helpful if litigation is involved—"

"Unpleasant for whom?" my father asks. "Us or you?"

Deputy Shin looks uncomfortable. "Both, sir, if I'm being honest. We've had trouble accessing these people in situations like this. They have good lawyers who will ensure we don't ever speak to their clients unless they're being arrested."

"You mean Seacrest people?" I ask. "They get to control their own narratives because they have money?"

Deputy Shin glances back at his younger partner. On cue, Deputy Williams straightens out of his cocky slouch and takes a step toward me. "We, uh, just have some questions for you concerning the whereabouts of Jackson Glanville. He's been reported missing."

"You have questions for *me*?"

"That's right, miss."

I let out a barking laugh. "I guess *we're* not the unpleasant ones around here. What do you want to know?"

Deputy Shin offers a placid smile. "We understand that you came to the station Saturday morning and spoke with one of our lieutenant deputies about Mr. Glanville."

I can feel my father staring at me. "That's correct."

"You also reported that you and Mr. Glanville 'had plans to meet at the Hollow Friday night' but that he didn't show."

"That's also right," I say.

Deputy Williams pipes up again. “So then what’d you do?”

“When?” I ask.

“When he didn’t show up at the place you’d planned to meet? What’d you do?”

“I tried calling him and texting. Multiple times. But he didn’t answer.”

“And after that?”

“Eventually I went home.”

“What time was this?” Deputy Williams asks.

“We were supposed to meet at eight forty-five.”

“No, what time did you get home that evening?”

I hesitate. “Is that important?”

“It might be. We’re trying to establish a timeline of his whereabouts.”

“My last contact with him was by phone Friday evening. We spoke at around eight fifteen and made plans to meet. That was it.”

The smirk returns to his face. “You sure about that?”

“What’re you getting at?” Dad asks.

Deputy Williams turns to look at him. “We’re just being thorough, sir.”

“I’m sure,” I say firmly. “That phone call was the last time I heard from him.”

The deputy nods. “So then what time’d you get home?”

“You already asked her that,” Dad growls from the couch.

Deputy Shin cuts in. “Sir, we’re just hoping to establish a clear sense of what occurred that night so that we can better understand the evidence we’ve found.”

My heart leaps. "What evidence?"

"Mr. Glanville's phone and wallet. They were found Sunday morning in the woods out past the Hollow. Right along the Ridge Trail, maybe a mile or so inland."

I gasp, my hand going to my mouth.

The older deputy watches me as he continues. "Now, that area isn't far from where you two intended to meet, so it would seem Mr. Glanville was out there recently. Most likely after you spoke with him Friday night. Unless . . ."

"Unless what?" I ask.

"Someone else had those items," he says.

"Why would someone have Jackson's phone and wallet?"

He shrugs. "Don't know. But there were several pairs of footprints that were found around where the items were located, so you can understand why we wondered if maybe you did see him later than you reported. Since, you know, he probably *was* in the woods that night and he wasn't alone."

My mind races, thinking back on that night, how I barreled into the woods after hearing what sounded like a struggle. So Jackson *was* out there? How close had I been to him? Who was he with?

And *why*?

"How'd you find them?" Dad asks.

Deputy Shin swivels in his direction. "Come again?"

"The phone and wallet. How'd you find them?"

"A GPS app," Deputy Williams says. "It'd been installed on his phone by his parents in case of emergency. Good thing, too."

"They're the emergency," I mutter. "They're the ones you should be looking at."

"Beatrice . . ." Dad warns.

Deputy Williams stares at me. "What was that?"

I fold my arms. "Nothing."

"So you don't really know when the phone got there," Dad clarifies. "It could've been Friday night after Bea spoke with him or any time up until Sunday morning."

"I suppose that's right." Although he's responding to my father, Deputy Shin has also turned around to meet my gaze, and there's no compassion in his expression anymore. Just a cool sort of interest. Like a hunting dog willing to wait out its prey. "Which is why it's so important for us to put this time-line together. It'll help answer a lot of questions."

"I see."

Now everyone's staring at me, awaiting my response, and my heart's rattling against my rib cage and my vision is narrowing because I can feel myself being led into a trap. I know better than to contradict what I told Lt. Deputy Bernstein on Saturday. When speaking to her, I purposely left out the chase in the woods and meeting up with the Broadmoor group. If I tried adding this info now, then I'd really look like the woman in the Sandra Cantu case.

The guilty one.

"I came right home," I announce. "I mean, I waited a while for him, and I called and texted like I told you. But I probably got back here around nine or nine-thirty. Ten at the very latest. It was homecoming and downtown was packed."

Deputies Shin and Williams exchange a skeptical look.

"You're sure?" the younger one asks. His smirk's completely gone now.

"Absolutely," I reply.

20

"I'M NOT SURE I UNDERSTAND what you're talking about," Dr. Wingate tells me on Tuesday afternoon when we meet for our weekly therapy session.

I shift around in the upholstered chair that I've come to think of as mine ever since that first day when I sank into it and tried so hard to disappear. With its large frame, overstuffed cushions, and thick turquoise fabric that's got enough heft for me to grip, it's the rare seat in which I feel safe. Protected.

Cared for.

Today, however, I'm harboring doubts. Or maybe I'm just resenting scrutiny at a time when people should be looking elsewhere. It *is* therapy, after all, and as always, Dr. Wingate is sitting across from me with his hands clasped and glasses on, and between us is this wide surfboard-shaped coffee table that's got a black racing stripe running down its center. Surrounding us are the framed black-and-white movie posters he's hung neatly around the room. I usually like how on brand they are, all psychological thrillers: *Marathon Man*, *The Boys from Brazil*, *The Manchurian Candidate*. Today, though, they leave me feeling paranoid.

I take a deep breath and look around, absorbing the space we're in as a way of fending off my nervous tunnel vision. I'm too old for the corner with the toys and sand tray table, but this room has always radiated with an appealing Bohemian warmth. More New Mexico than New England, and I appreciate the sense of earthy optimism and whole-hearted rejection of what passes for tradition in this town—tacky whitewashed flooring, beadboard wainscoting, and piles of Colonial clutter. The only nods to Dr. Wingate's medical roots are his framed degree from Dartmouth and a bound manuscript titled "The Overreaches of Medical Research: A History" that sits on the corner of his desk—his thesis, I assume.

"Wait, what don't you understand?" I finally say, although it's clear my mind is elsewhere. "I'm sorry. What *were* we talking about?"

"You were telling me that you lied to the police about your whereabouts Friday night. And that Evie's angry with you because you didn't tell her about Jackson being missing. There was also some miscommunication with this Carlos person. By your report it would seem there's a lot of deception going on in your life right now, but I want to make sure I'm understanding the situation correctly."

"Oh, I think you understand everything about as well as I do," I chirp.

Dr. Wingate makes one of his *uh-huh* noises, which I know means he's frustrated. "Then I guess I'm also confused about the part where Evie said she doesn't believe that you're even friends with Jackson anymore. *Are* you two friends? You and Jackson?"

"Of course." My tone is indignant. "Why do you think I wanted him to see you?"

"So, then how do you understand Evie's reaction?"

I bite my lip, thinking of the way she just straight up ignored me in the hall at school today. Roo and Dane followed suit because, like me, that's ultimately what they are: followers of a higher power. "I don't know. It was an honest reaction, and I can see her point. She was there for me when he and I stopped being friends and it probably hurt her to find out that that wasn't true anymore."

"Is *that* what hurt her? Or is it the fact that you kept your repaired friendship with Jackson a secret from her?"

"I only did that because Jax is so private! I never wanted to break his confidence."

"You're very protective of him."

"Someone has to be. Plus, you're the one who told me about privacy. That it's wrong to disclose information about another person's personal life without their permission."

"Unless it's an emergency," Dr. Wingate adds. "Which this is."

"I *know*. That's why I reported him missing. But I also tried to keep the details to a minimum, and now no one believes anything I have to say. Or that I even *have* something to say. Because it's not like I have proof of what we talked about. Why would I? All I ever wanted was to help him. To make up for what I did."

"Maybe he knew that," Dr. Wingate says softly, his blue eyes piercing straight into my core.

"What do you mean?"

"I mean maybe Jackson knew your guilt would keep you from saying anything about him. And *that's* the reason he felt safe getting close to you again."

"That's pretty messed up," I say.

"From what you've said, he's been dealing with a lot." Dr. Wingate pauses. "Couldn't you report what you know now? Everything that happened to you Friday night?"

I pick at the spot on the chair arm where a knot of fabric's pulled loose. "Can you imagine, after the fact, someone saying, 'By the way, I didn't tell you earlier, but I thought I heard someone in the woods the night my friend disappeared. I tried following them but then they ended up chasing me until I was rescued by some random strangers'? It's not very convincing. It sounds like . . ."

"Like what?"

I look up. "Like I've got something to hide."

Dr. Wingate tips his head back, steeples his fingers. "How much are you sleeping these days, Bea?"

"I don't know."

"Six hours? Eight?"

I hedge. "Four? On a good night."

"Are you still having that same dream?"

I nod. "Is that weird? It doesn't feel weird. Seeing him in the dream is almost comforting since I can't stop thinking about him anyway."

"Why do you think that is?"

"Because he's missing? Because someone might have abducted him? Or worse?"

"No, I mean, why this dream? Why now?"

I tilt my head. What an odd question. "It's always been this dream. Whenever I'm stressed, it comes back."

"Okay."

I scoot my butt forward and sit up. "But honestly, it kind of makes sense, if you think about it. The dream is about something terrible happening to Jackson. Only I've always thought it was about the past. Something his grandfather did that might've put Jackson at risk. But what if this whole time the dream has been about the present? What if it's about *now*?"

"Like a premonition?" Dr. Wingate lifts a concerned brow.

"It doesn't matter what it's called."

"Aren't you children in the dream?"

"Maybe it's not meant to be literal."

"Maybe it's just a dream," he says. "An artifact of your generalized worries, experiences, and emotions. Nothing more."

My jaw tightens. "Thanks for believing in me."

"I didn't say I don't believe in you, Beatrice. I'm just not sure that entertaining the notion that your dreams are prescient is ultimately going to be helpful to you."

"I'm not trying to help *me*!" I cry out. "I want to find Jackson!"

Dr. Wingate leans forward. "I understand how frightening it is to not know where your friend is. But at the end of the day, *you're* my client. And I'm worried about you."

"Why?" I ask.

"Because you're putting the responsibility of saving Jackson entirely on your shoulders."

"Okay."

"It's not okay. It's not healthy. It's also a little . . ."

"A little what?"

"Fatalistic," he says. "If you believe you're responsible for saving your friend, what will that mean if you fail?"

"You think I'm going to fail?" I ask.

"Beatrice," he says. "You need to take care of yourself."

"I *am.*"

"Because that's the other side of fatalism, you know. If you believe saving Jackson is your destiny, then that belief can lead to other consequences."

"Like what?"

"Risk taking. Putting yourself in danger. Real danger. You've already told me a girl died."

"Is that all?" I ask. I mean, I'm not worried about *dying.* That feels like an overreach.

"I need to know you can be safe."

And I need to know my friend will come back, I long to say. Instead, I tap my fingers against the chair arm. "I promise I'll be safe."

"Okay."

"Hey, I solved that case, you know. The old one I've been writing about in my column. Chrissy Lambert? Turns out it wasn't a murder."

His expression is puzzled. "What?"

"Don't you read my column?"

"Only when you ask me to. I don't regularly involve myself in my clients' lives outside of our sessions. I fear it might be experienced as intrusive."

I roll my eyes. "You want to know how I know you don't have kids?"

Dr. Wingate winces.

"I'm sorry," I say quickly.

"It's not your fault."

No, it's not, but I still feel bad. "Look, I always want you to read my stuff. I really mean that. Especially the one I'm going to write tonight."

"Then I will," he says.

HOME ABOUT NEWS ARCHIVE

TRUEMAINE.COM

Home Page for the State of Maine . . . and Murder

"A Void"

In my last column, I wrote about the impact Chrissy Lambert's death had on Cabot Cove. How the town's anxiety and fear over this unsolved crime spurred its citizens to action—all in the name of keeping their children safe.

Now I won't argue that the thought of a killer on the loose is terrifying. It's a reality that pretty much cries out for *someone to do something.* So maybe it's understandable that it was in this void that factions formed, groups of people all seeking to convince the town that *they* were the ones who could keep the children safe. In return, the town rewarded them with money.

And power.

In a mystery novel, such reward might also be called a motive. Find who has the most to gain and you'll often find a killer. Still, it's hard to believe that members of a neighborhood Crime Watch group or the Sheriff's Office or even school board members would go so far as to murder Chrissy in order to enrich their causes.

But what if the real motive were the same, only more personal? What if there was someone in her life who felt so deeply that Chrissy needed protection from the outside world that they ended up hurting her?

What if that person was her father?

Chrissy Lambert died by suicide. This is the tragic truth of what happened in the Ocean View Country Club ballroom on the night of her father's birthday party. And while suicide is a complex, multifaceted act that often defies easy explanations or understanding, we do have Chrissy's own words to offer a window into her state of mind that evening (see photo A—inset).

We also have her father's actions in the aftermath. Using his power and wealth and his position as the town mayor, he covered up Chrissy's suicide and conspired to have a second medical examiner label her death as strangulation (see photo B). He must have also conspired with the other wealthy party guests and witnesses to never speak the truth about his daughter's final moments.

Personally, I think there was nothing noble in his choices. By running off his daughter's boyfriend, Chrissy's father wasn't looking to spare her reputation—only his own. And just as he worked to rewrite her romantic options, he also rewrote her death, erasing her truth and casting her as the victim of someone, anyone, who wasn't him.

So in the end, Chrissy Lambert wasn't a murder victim. At least not in the way we thought. But I guess what I still don't understand is *why*? Not why did her father do the things he did, but why did he feel so free to do them? Where does that impulse come from? And what void was he seeking to fill?

Feel free to enlighten me in the comments.

Yours truly,

—the Downeast Girl

Sign up for our newsletter!

21

WALKING TO SCHOOL THE FOLLOWING morning, I brace myself for both Evie's ire and more rumors spawned by the column I posted last night, which I only felt comfortable doing after Aaron reassured me that my piece was fine. More than fine, he'd said, it was "actually kind of outstanding." According to him, the site really wants me to keep writing and researching and doing exactly what I'm doing, which I guess means solving old mysteries with definitive answers. "Just stay away from current events," he warned, and I agreed, even though the past has lost its luster of late. The present is what I care about.

The only thing.

Around me, leaves shimmer with peak color. Showy and bright, some grip to their branches to light the sky above me, and those that don't crunch beneath my shoes. As I walk, I'm hit by a surge of nostalgia and longing so strong that for an instant, the world around me fades from focus. It's a feeling I've had before, something intangible that lives within fleeting moments of beauty and change and a future that gapes wide ahead of me.

My breath grows ragged and sad, but I hold myself

upright and slip through the high school's main gate before skirting the gravel parking lot and drop-off area that's already lined with idling cars and pickups. CCH doesn't have the regal presence of Broadmoor Castle, but it's a well-kept school, nestled on the east side of town and backing up against our largest city park. The main classroom buildings are all brick and stately, with high slanted roofs; beneath them runs a dingy network of underground walkways that keep us out of the elements during winter. Between the buildings sits a wind-shielded patio, creatively dubbed the Quad, which is where students tend to gather between classes during the months when the weather permits.

Stepping onto school property, the first thing I notice are the decorations. Honestly, they're hard *not* to notice. Overnight, it appears that whatever student group's in charge of such things has plastered every available space with bright orange-and-black signs advertising Cabot Cove's annual "Carnoween" celebration, which is held downtown on the night before Halloween and consists of carnival games, cheap rides, a bad DJ, and lots of free candy. Even our school's big marquee sign, which had spelled out HAPPY HOMECOMING, DEVILS for the past few weeks, has been altered to read: TEN MORE DAYS 'TIL CARNOWEEN!

I roll my eyes at the heavy-handed marketing push. Carnoween's a huge hit with the grade school crowd. But every year, the town puts out this hard sell to the teens, and every year their efforts fail horribly. Because Halloween Eve is Cabbage Night, aka Mischief Night aka the night when local high schoolers run wild through the town and raise some (mostly harmless) hell. Pranks usually consist of nuisances like toilet papering, egg throwing, exploding pumpkins, and maybe the occasional stink bomb or mailbox smashing. Annoying, sure, but the way our boomer population responds, you'd think we'd unleashed the Purge. You'd also think they hadn't done the exact same thing when they were our age.

Once inside, I savor the humming radiator warmth and make my way to my first-floor locker. Through a series of wide plateglass windows, I take note of what's going on in the Quad—the yearly scarecrows have been assembled for the Spooky Scare contest. Now this is a *real* Cabot Cove High tradition. Every October, tons of hay bales and pumpkins are trucked in, and each class is responsible for setting up an elaborate scene featuring some sort of Halloween-themed scarecrow. These are later judged for prizes, and the field is highly competitive. Already, a small crowd has gathered, so it's probably worth a peek. After grabbing my books—today's a block schedule day and I've got English and pre-calc before lunch—I go to check out the displays.

Falling in line with other interested students, I shuffle along the inside perimeter of the Quad. First up is the freshman scarecrow, which is goofy, and I mean that literally because he's wearing a Goofy T-shirt and a droopy-eared hat. Sitting beside him is a snaggle-toothed taxidermied raccoon that appears to have been afflicted with mange—either before or after its demise—and the sense one gets is that the scarecrow and raccoon are lost in deep conversation.

Bizarrely, other strange animal carcasses and rubber mice are scattered across the scene.

"Gross," a girl behind me says.

Biting back a smile, I move on to the senior scarecrow, which clearly had a bigger budget and grander vision. This one is done up as a scene from the folk horror film *Midsommar*. The scarecrow is dressed as a man dressed as a bear, and is draped in what looks alarmingly like a genuine bearskin. Pagan-like symbols have been spray-painted across the hay bales, and the scarecrow's feet are surrounded by cut-out cardboard flames wrapped in aluminum foil. The faux flames are illuminated by battery-operated candles, casting an eerie metallic glow in the morning light.

The girl behind me says nothing, which I think says it all. The scene's truly grotesque, and this one's got my vote, so far.

Next is the junior class effort, which is my class, and I stop dead in front of the scarecrow, perplexed by its simplicity. People are actually passing it by because there's really nothing to see. Super low effort. Our scarecrow consists of a pile of cheap orange Hefty bags stuffed with leaves, topped with a pumpkin, and it's wearing a Cabot Cove High athletic uniform—a red-and-gold jersey and shorts. Although upon further inspection, I notice that the scarecrow's holding a basketball in its lap, only the ball is black and has wires dangling from it. Which is strange. Then it hits me—it's not a ball at all.

The scarecrow's holding a fake *bomb*.

With a whimper, I press closer, knees brushing up

against the bales, until I spot the red stains smearing the scarecrow's jersey, dotting the shorts. Looking down, I see a dark liquid pooling from beneath the hay as well as a small white note card. I have to squint to read it, but scrawled in red lettering across the note card is the message:

MEET ME AT THE HOLLOW . . .

A lump forms in my throat, my breath grows shallow, and it's almost as if I've floated outside of myself. As if I'm hovering in the air and watching my own body swipe and push past other students in an effort to step around to take in the back of the display. Although I already know what I'm going to see.

Still, anticipation doesn't numb the utter revulsion I feel when I finally get a good look and actually shriek out loud, making everyone around me turn and stare.

A number and a name are printed on the back of the scarecrow's basketball jersey:

15

Glanville

It's *Jackson's*.

22

“HOLY CRAP.” LEISL’S EYES WIDEN with increasing alarm as I recount the scarecrow story to her at a picnic table outside Moe’s Seafood Shack later that afternoon. “Someone at your school actually did that? Why? Who was it?”

“I don’t know.” I push my fried artichokes away. “Turns out it wasn’t even the scarecrow our class committee had made. Someone moved theirs overnight and the committee was pretty upset about it. The one they made was this Pennywise spider clown thing, and someone hid it in the girls’ locker room.”

“Sadists,” Leisl says.

I give a dispirited shrug. “I guess. I mean, it’s just a stupid joke.”

“You think it was a *joke*? What was the punch line?”

“To scare people?”

“That’s not very funny.” Leisl picks at her lobster roll. “Are you sure you’re okay? We don’t have to do this right now. Our research sharing can wait until later.”

“I don’t think it can,” I say.

“Then why don’t I go first?” Leisl flips her hair back and straightens her spine before tossing a piece of bread at a row of seagulls on the next picnic table over. "Oh, look. A feeding frenzy."

"Moe's going to kill you." I point to one of the highly visible signs that reads: DO NOT FEED THE BIRDS NO MATTER HOW MUCH THEY BEG AND BOTHER YOU. I KNOW YOU'VE READ THIS.

She waves dismissively. "Whatever. You ready?"

"Absolutely."

"Okay, so I was really curious about what you told me about the Seacrest Homeowners Association and how their influence extends to the entire town. Not just their neighborhood or personal property. In order to understand this better, I consulted with my dad, who happens to be in a legal profession."

She reaches down to pull a tidy Moleskine from her side bag and begins to scan the pages. "First off, he told me that this HOA's actions sounded irregular, but not unheard of. Apparently to understand the true scope of their power, we'd have to look at how the group was initially established, which goes back to your shadow government thing."

"What do you mean?" I ask.

"Well, most HOAs are established when a new housing development is being built. Dues and membership are a requirement when someone purchases a home. But this HOA was established long after this neighborhood had been built, meaning there was nothing in these homeowners' deeds obligating them—financially or otherwise—to join an HOA. Unless . . ."

"Yes?"

"Unless they agreed to amend their deeds after the fact.

That's possible. But it would be weird. Why give up autonomy if you don't have to?"

"Is that what they did?" I ask.

"We don't know. Maybe the people in charge sincerely convinced all their neighbors that signing on would be in their best interest. Or maybe they twisted some arms to get people on board. Then there's a third option: that they're not really an HOA at all, but more of a political party."

A chill comes over me. "Like maybe the whole group's a fraud?"

"Maybe," she admits. "I'd have to look into it more to find out. But I can ask my dad about that."

"Thanks."

"What did you learn?"

"Yeah, well, given what you've just told me, I think you'll find this pretty interesting." I reach for my own notebook that's already out on the picnic table, only slightly splattered with cocktail sauce. Opening to the relevant page, I hold it out to Leisl and point. Written down, in my god-awful handwriting, are the names of all the missing teens, minus Eden.

TRENT MICHAELS
IRIS MULVANEY
BENSON HORACE
JACKSON GLANVILLE

"Guess the connection between them," I urge.

Her brow furrows. "Three boys and a girl? Are they Irish?"

"Irish? What? No, they're from Seacrest. All of them. I looked it up on their website."

"So they're all from the same neighborhood? The one with the HOA? That can't be a coincidence."

"That's not all," I say. "In the last two years, all of their mothers have served on the HOA's board. Well, not Iris's, actually. But her mom's listed as the email coordinator, which feels close enough. She's involved and they only moved back to Cabot Cove a year ago. Her mom grew up here, though."

"Moved back from where?"

"Kennebunk. It's not far. Just down the coast a piece."

Leisl snickers. "A piece."

"Always with the jokes," I tell her.

"It's the natural consequence of having an obnoxious brother." She sticks a fry in her mouth. "So did you know them? The missing kids?"

"Kind of. Iris I had a class with last year. English. Trent and Benson are both a grade ahead of me, but I know who they are. Trent had a reputation for doing a lot of drugs. He missed school a lot, so who knows. Benson's a musician. He plays cello and piano. He used to be involved in the local orchestra, but he quit at some point."

"Why?"

"Got sick of it, I guess. His whole life was spent practicing."

"How did they disappear?"

"I don't know. It wasn't like it made the news. They were just gone."

"Are you sure they were actually reported missing?"

"Well, there were flyers with their photos posted in the Sheriff's Office, so yeah, someone reported something. But it feels like the bare minimum, you know?" I try and recall why the flyers struck me as so odd. "It was like the photos weren't even that recent. Although Seacrest families have a habit of doing things their own way and shutting out law enforcement. They might not have gone the official route and hired private investigators instead."

"I see." Leisl frowns.

"What's wrong?" I ask.

"Well, if it were *my* kid and they were missing, I'd tell everyone. No way would I keep that a secret. I'd tell the cops and private investigators and the FBI and all the kids on TikTok. I'd get on TV and talk to Nancy Grace and shout to the whole entire world what was going on. As much as I could. I wouldn't stop. Unless—"

"Unless you'd been told not to," I finish. "Of *course.* These are rich kids. Their families have a ton of money. You think they're being held for ransom? Is that possible? Or maybe blackmail?"

"I don't know. But this group, the way you've described them, I bet they have a lot of enemies."

I nod, my mind spinning with possibilities. "True."

"I wish we knew more about the circumstances of how they disappeared." Leisl drums her fingers on the table. "Do you think there's anyone else we could talk with? Do any of the missing teens have siblings?"

"Iris does," I say slowly. "A little brother."

23

LEISL DOESN'T HAVE A BIKE, so I have to walk beside mine and push it the whole way over to Seacrest. It's a hassle, but after what happened this morning with the scarecrow, I'm mostly grateful not to be alone with my fears and my worries. My runaway brain.

Who would do something like that?

What if they don't get what they want?

What then?

"This town's bigger than I imagined." Leisl's head keeps swiveling as we cut through downtown Cabot Cove, taking in the different stores and crowds. An afternoon farmers market near the courthouse is crowded with people buying pumpkins and cocoa and organic lettuces. "Driving up to Broadmoor, you don't see any of this."

"You don't ever come down here on your own?"

"Not really."

"Why'd you decide to go to boarding school?" I ask. "Was that something you wanted to do? Or was it your parents' choice?"

Leisl smooths her hair, blown wild by the wind. "Well,

I didn't want to stay in Branford, Connecticut, if that's what you're asking."

"Is it worse than Maine?"

"Maine's not bad," she says.

"In the summer, maybe."

She pulls at the straps of the dark overalls she's wearing. "Let's put it this way—I'm a romantic. Living in a secluded castle surrounded by snow is pretty much my ideal aesthetic. Even if arguing with other rich kids about Dante and Milton doesn't teach me anything about living in the real world."

"Milton, huh?" I say slowly, turning a thought over in my mind.

"Oh, here's a thing about boarding school that no one tells you," Leisl continues. "It's a good chance to start over. To reinvent yourself in whatever fantasy fills your mind. There's a lot to be said for running away from one's problems."

"What problems are you running away from?"

Leisl laughs. "In my case, it'd be more accurate to say I'm running from my brother's. Or that he's the one doing the running. I'm just along for the ride."

"Leif? What did he do?"

She turns and grips my arm. "I'm sorry. I know I talk a lot. It's annoying."

"No, it's not. I like hearing you talk. It's helping to distract me. Say something more."

"You're really worried, huh?"

"Yes."

She nods. "I'll keep talking then. You asked about Milton, right? He's practically our school's mascot."

"He is?"

"Absolutely."

"Have you heard of the uncouth swain?" I venture.

Leisl stops dead center in the middle of the road, closes her eyes, and holds one hand to her heart. She recites:

"'Thus sang the uncouth swain to th'oaks and rills,
While the still morn went out with sandals gray;
He touch'd the tender stops of various quills,
With eager thought warbling his Doric lay;'"

I clap loudly when she's finished, nearly dropping my bike in the process. "I guess you really do know Milton."

She opens her eyes. "That imagery's pretty phallic but it's way better than Byron's rosy-cheeked lasses. I hate Byron. But why're you asking about *Lycidas*?"

"I told you. The uncouth swain is the name of the person who left the comment on my article last weekend. 'The hungry sheep look up and are not fed?'"

"You didn't tell me that," she says.

I'm pretty sure I did.

Leisl starts walking again, as we approach the turnoff to Seacrest Drive. "So does this swain actually have a connection to your friend? Or any of the other missing teens?"

I scramble after her. "I don't know. Whoever it is, they're

paranoid about surveillance, which tracks with this all-knowing HOA stuff. I told you about the private security guards, but did you know Jackson's parents monitored his phone and internet history? Though it's always possible the swain is more interested in Chrissy Lambert than Jackson."

"Oooh!" she exclaims. "I forgot to tell you that I looked into him! Chrissy's secret MIT boyfriend. Okay, well, mostly I forgot because I haven't found anything yet, but I think I know where to look."

"Where's that?"

"There's this room in the top of our library where the school keeps all their alumni stuff. Apparently, they've got copies of every yearbook ever in there. We know this guy's name starts with *A*, and if he was run off by Chrissy's dad for being poor, he might've been a Trustee Scholar. Broadmoor gives out two full-ride scholarships a year to students, and there's usually a picture of them."

"It's worth a shot." I agree. "Can you get in?"

"I think so. The room's locked, but the library calls it a 'historical collection,' which means it's open for public viewing. I just need to get the key. Oh, and you know what else is in there? *Whale heads.*"

"Excuse me?"

"They're from our actual mascot costume. Not Milton, but Nova. Oh, come on, you know her." Leisl looks incredulous as I shake my head. "She's *Nova*, the humpback whale. Anyway, they've got all the original costume heads stored in that room. It sounds *awesome.*"

"It sounds terrifying," I tell her.

The Seacrest guardhouse comes into view, blocking entry into the winding coastal neighborhood. I jog forward with my bike and rap on the window with my knuckles. When it slides open, the woman inside isn't anyone I recognize.

"Yes," she says curtly.

"My friend and I are coming to visit the Mulvaneys."

"Are you residents?"

"Of Cabot Cove. Not Seacrest."

"You got ID?"

"No one's ever asked for that before."

"Security's being stepped up," she says. "Not sure why."

I pull out my wallet, show her my school ID, then nod at Leisl. "She's with me."

The woman scowls. "I need a name."

Leisl steps forward. "I'm Leisl Schoenholz."

The woman pauses. "Schoenholz? You mean—"

"That's right."

"Well, welcome," she says in an awed kind of voice.

The gate arm immediately lifts, and we thank her and walk in. I turn to Leisl.

"What was that?" I ask. "Who *are* you?"

Her jaw tightens. "It's not me. It's my father. Bruce Schoenholz. I told you, he's a lawyer. He teaches constitutional law at Yale."

"Oh." I consider this. "But is he famous? Like, does he represent celebrities? Or serial killers? Why would a random person on the street know who he was?"

"I don't think most random people would. But she"—Leisl jabs her thumb back at the guardhouse—"was studying for the LSAT. She had a prep guide out. So she definitely knows his name."

"Your dad's in the LSAT prep guide?"

"Yup. But no, he doesn't represent celebrities or serial killers. Unless you count politicians."

I stop walking. "Then what are these cases that are so famous they're studied in law school?"

She glances back at me with a wry smile, one belying her usual aura of carefree disinterest. "Oh, just ones he's argued before the Supreme Court. And won."

24

WE STARE UP AT THE Mulvaney house. Although modest in comparison to the Glanvilles' snow globe spectacular, the large home oozes opulence and means but also a deep sense of foreboding. Situated on a lush lot backing up to a bird sanctuary, it's built in the Dutch Colonial style, replete with twin dormers, a massive sun porch, and one of those leering gambrel rooflines. More than anything it reminds me of *The Amityville Horror*. It feels like the house is looking at us looking at it.

I don't like it.

"You know these people?" Leisl asks in a hushed voice.

"Not really. Like I said, I knew Iris a little bit, but she was only in school with me for six months or so. Then she was just gone, and no one ever said a word about it.'"

"That's so sad."

"Yeah, it is."

"Uh-oh." Leisl points. "Someone's watching us."

I follow her gaze and she's right. A child, a young messy-haired boy, has snuck around from the back of the Mulvaneys' house and is currently watching us with binoculars from behind a large landscaping boulder.

"That's Iris's little brother. I forget his name." I quickly wave at him then tug Leisl's arm. "Come on. We better talk to him before anyone else shows up."

We step into the front yard, a lush maze of winding paths that guide us past beds of feathery seagrass and other hardy native plants. Approaching the house, the ocean comes into view from the back and over the bluff in the distance—a shining stretch of sparkling water and nothing beyond.

The boy with the binoculars vanishes momentarily, slipping behind the boulder before reappearing near a free-standing pergola draped in ivy on the western side of the house.

I wave again and call out. "What's your name? I'm Beatrice."

"I'm Perry," he calls back.

"Can we talk to you for a minute, Perry?"

"Sure." The boy leans against the pergola as we approach.

"Thanks," I say as I we reach him.

"Can I ride your bike?" he asks.

"Can we talk first? We'll be quick. I promise."

"They're watching us, you know," he says. "That's why I'm out here."

"*Who's* watching you?" Leisl asks. "Your parents?"

The boy creeps forward and then, without saying a word, he very delicately takes hold of my bike's handles, pushing it from beneath my grasp before I even realize what's happening. He swings onto the seat and wobbles around the flagstone patio for a bit before putting his leg down. He's a young kid, maybe nine or ten, and he stares at Leisl with very serious eyes.

"Who are you?" he asks.

She smiles. "My name's Leisl."

"That's a boy's name."

"That's true. It can be a boy's name. But it can be my name, too."

"You can sit if you want." Sliding off the bike and lowering it to the ground, Perry gestures at a pair of glossy red Adirondack chairs that have been positioned to face the ocean. Leisl and I oblige.

"Okay, now watch this," he says, darting out of sight. "Just hold on."

"Do you like little kids?" Leisl asks me.

"I don't know," I say, and right then there's this huge whooshing sound and a giant flame shoots out of the ground in front of us.

Leisl shrieks while I cover my eyes. When I open them again, Perry's returned.

"It's a firepit," he says scornfully. "It's supposed to keep you warm."

"I think it needs a childproof lock," Leisl mutters.

"I go to school with your sister," I say. "Or I did. I'm sorry that she's missing."

Perry wrinkles his nose. "Iris isn't missing. She's just not here."

"So where is she?"

"Mom says she's in trouble. That she better come back before it's too late."

"What does that mean?"

"You know."

"You mean she's pregnant?" Leisl ventures.

Perry's eyebrows go up. "How would that happen?"

I poke Leisl in the side and shake my head sternly. "Where do *you* think your sister is, Perry?"

He gestures vaguely. "In the woods."

"She lives in the woods?"

"With the owls. She'll come back, though. She told me."

"When did you last see her?"

"I don't know."

"How are your parents doing?"

"Uh-oh." Perry points behind me. I turn to look and see that one of the Seacrest private security guard vehicles has pulled up to the curb.

"Damn it," I say. "What're they doing?"

"Stay here." Perry darts off again, leaving us alone to face the authorities.

"Let me talk to them." Leisl rises slowly from her Adirondack chair.

"Use your legal knowledge," I mutter to her. *And your whiteness.* I watch as Leisl smooths her long hair, smiles, waves, and bounces straight toward the uniformed guard as he's stepping out of his car. It's kind of masterful to watch. Her approach doesn't come from a place of entitlement or *I will not stand for this* rage but rather utter bewilderment. It's more like, surely someone like him has no reason to speak with someone like her, and she treats his presence like a novelty.

A gift, really.

I look back and spot Perry slipping out from under the front porch, his knees coated in dirt and rock dust. He's holding something in his hand. I beckon for him by hooking my finger, and he barrels over, eyes gleaming with satisfaction.

"What were you doing?" I ask. "No more fires, right?"

"Here." The small boy's so close, I can feel his breath, warm against my cheek. He slides something at me, slipping it into the folds of my jacket. My back is to the others, and I slide it down my waistband and under my shirt.

"What is it?" I whisper.

"She wants you to have it."

"Who? Your sister?"

"Shh." He puts a finger to his lips. "I already told you. They're watching."

×××

In our eagerness to flee Seacrest post–security guard altercation, I let Leisl ride double on the bike with me through the marshland trails. This is a terrible idea, as I basically have to stand while pedaling as she grips onto my waist in an effort not to fall off backward. We nearly go down multiple times, but the bike path's downhill and once we get going, we fly.

"What'd you tell him?" I shout.

She laughs. Holds on tighter. "Nothing!" she shouts back, her voice whipping in the wind.

"No, really. They're notorious hard-asses out here."

"I get that," she shouts. "But I didn't say anything to him to get him to stop harassing us. I just answered every question with a question until he gave up."

"But what kind of questions? You name-drop Daddy again?"

She pinches me, hard, which causes me to swerve off the path and onto the soft dirt, where the front wheel skids out, sending us both crashing to the ground.

"You deserved that," Leisl scolds.

"I'm sorry."

She reaches out and takes my hand, pulls me up to sitting. "You should let people keep their secrets."

"That's a lesson I keep learning. And unlearning."

"For instance—"

"Are you bleeding?" I point to her elbow where her sweater's been torn and the skin beneath it looks ragged and filthy.

"Hey, what's that?" The tenor of her voice changes and I look to see the red envelope on the ground, apparently having shot from my waist during the crash.

"Perry gave it to me." Even before I'm done speaking, Leisl's lunging for the envelope, pulling it to her.

"Can I open it?" she asks. I nod and she scoots back, pressing her spine against the bike path guardrail. I unclip my helmet and settle beside her. We both pull our knees up tight, shielding the envelope from the wind.

Leisl uses a perfectly buffed nail to gently pry it open. She doesn't tear or rip and there's such deliberateness in her effort I can tell she's done this before. Finally, she loosens the glued triangle flap and pulls it back. Then she presses gently on both sides of the envelope, compressing it just enough so that she's able to peek inside. Frowning, she holds it out to me, and I peer at the contents.

"What is that?" I ask. I can make out two small laminated cards but also, lining the bottom of the envelope, is some kind of substance. Something pale and dusty.

"Hold out your hand," Leisl orders.

I stare at her. "What if it's anthrax? Or ricin?"

"Just trust me."

So I do. I hold out my cupped sweaty hand and watch as she tips a handful of what looks like horse feed into it.

"Are these oats?" I ask, picking one up and holding it close.

"Looks like it. Pretty weird, huh?" Leisl scoops out the two cards from the envelope and sets them on her thighs. Each has a black-and-white illustration that looks like it was plucked from a biology textbook. The first is of a brain. Human, I assume. The second is of a hand.

"Oats, brain, and a hand," I say. "This is a clue, right? We've moved on from the posse comitatus to the church to Chrissy's suicide note to . . . this?"

The faintest hint of a smile reaches her lips.

"That's right," she says. "It's a clue."

"But *how*? How could that kid, whose sister is genuinely missing, possibly abducted by *owls*, have this?"

"That's right, he said owls. Do you think he meant something witchy? Like a child-stealing witch?"

"That's not funny," I say.

"I'm not trying to be funny. I'm trying to figure this out."

"But who gave him the clue?"

"I don't know. We need to think about this strategically."

I nod but can't help feeling frustrated. Isn't this what I *am* doing? Being strategic and thinking creatively? The thing is, I'm not sure who to trust or even how, because here I am, getting entwined in riddles and poems and suicide notes. With ugly scarecrows and beautiful girls and soft-spoken boys who drink their coffee with cream. But around every corner, there's never an answer.

Only more questions.

25

I DROP LEISL OFF AT the shuttle stop, where she's able to catch a ride back to Broadmoor.

"I hate taking this thing," she confesses.

"Because it's public transportation?"

She sighs. "You really think the worst of me, don't you?"

"I don't know what to think. Why do you hate it?" I ask.

"The driver's always wearing these creepy leather gloves. Like a pervert. Sunglasses, too. Oh, and he calls me 'little lady.'"

I laugh. "That's pretty bad. I agree."

"I'll call you tomorrow, all right? Or you call me."

"It's a date," I tell her, to which she raises an eyebrow.

"Then I definitely won't tell the boys about it," she says with a grin.

My heart flutters around a little as I hop on my bike and head toward home. It's closing in on sundown, but there's enough light left that I'm not risking my life or anything. My left knee acts up a little, sharp twinges of pain I feel on the inclines. Probably a result of when we fell on the side of the road. I smile at the image of us both flying into the dirt.

It's nearly dark by the time I turn onto our street and cruise toward our house. It's surrounded by a purply gloom of trees and shadows and nestled beneath the velvet sky. I brake at the curb and swing off, surprised to see lights on inside. Dad's home early, which sets my nerves on edge. That certainly hasn't been the norm this week. After unclipping my helmet, I hoist the bike onto the sidewalk and push through our front gate. As I enter the yard, I sense movement near a row of unclipped hedges.

Startled, I hold the bike in front of me. "Is someone there?"

"Hey," a voice says from the darkness. "Don't freak out. I just want to talk to you."

"Who are you? I'll scream if you don't tell me who you are."

Holding their hands up, the person steps from the shadows into the warm glow radiating from our living room window. I gasp. It's *Deputy Williams*—the smirking young officer I met with earlier in the week. Only this time he's alone. Just hiding in the bushes.

Just waiting to ambush me.

"What're you doing?" I ask.

"Look, I have to tell you something." Unlike the other night, Deputy Williams looks nervous. His pale face is shiny with sweat.

I risk a glance at the window above us, willing my father to look out. To rescue me. "You wanted to tell *me* something?"

"That's right." His voice is low, gruff.

"Where's your partner?"

Deputy Williams takes another step forward, lurching toward me like a robot.

"Stop moving." I snap.

He stops. Tilts his head. "You don't remember me, do you?"

I shiver. "Of course I remember you. You were just at my house the other night."

"That's not what I mean."

"Then tell me what you mean."

"You don't have to be so nasty," he says. "I came here to help you."

"With what?"

"You were at the Mulvaneys' today, weren't you?"

"How could you know that?" Then it hits me. "Wait, did that security officer tell you we were there?"

He snorts. "Those rent-a-cops? No. They're not your friend and they're not mine either. I'm talking about you figuring out what's really going down on that side of town. Things no one wants you or me to know. They're a lot of unsettled scores around here."

"Is this about the scarecrow?" I ask.

Deputy Williams curls his lip. "What're you talking about?"

"At the high school this morning. Someone dressed up a scarecrow to look like Jackson Glanville. They had his basketball uniform, the one with his name on it, and blood was smeared all over it. Only instead of a basketball, the scarecrow was holding a fake bomb."

"A fake bomb?" he echoes.

"It's a reference to his grandfather."

"Yeah, I get it. I know who the kid's grandfather was."

"But that's not why you're here," I say.

"No."

"Then why?"

"It's those missing kids. You're right, you know. There's something's screwed up about it. I don't have the clearance to look at their files, so I tried asking my partner, the lieutenant deputy, even the sheriff—they all tell me to drop it. Three—four missing kids, all from Seacrest, the richest neighborhood around, and no one wants to acknowledge it's happening. It's like . . ."

"Like what?"

His eyes dart around, looking every which way. "It's like they're *scared* to look into it."

"So you've noticed they're from Seacrest. But did you also notice that their moms are all involved with the HOA board? That's a pretty powerful group. Maybe powerful enough to get an investigation shut down."

"An investigation *to find their children*?" His expression is incredulous.

"I don't know!" I exclaim. "What do you want me to do about it?"

"Keep looking into it! For that column you write. Find the truth. Figure out what's happening. Expose it. That's what you do, isn't it? Online?"

"You know about my column?" I ask.

"Yeah, sure," he says.

"But it's anonymous."

Deputy Williams gives me a death stare. "Bea. I'm a detective."

"Are you the uncouth swain?"

"Who?"

"Never mind."

That little smirk appears on the deputy's face again. "So you gonna look into this or what?"

"I'm trying! But I don't know what I can do that you can't. I'm in *high school.*"

"Oh, you can do a lot, Miss Fletcher." Deputy Williams takes a step back. "Look, I've gotta go. But we'll talk soon."

"We will? When? How?"

He shakes his head. "You really don't remember me, do you?"

"How would I remember you?"

He retreats into the night. "Ask your rich friends. They'll know."

× × ×

I'm still shaking as I dash up the steps and fumble my way inside. I lock the door behind me as my father calls my name. He's in the kitchen, so that's where I go.

Dad's decked out in his navy fleece sweats, bopping around, making food, as Ella Fitzgerald streams from the wireless speaker he's hung from the pot rack. My heart swells at the sight of him, with fondness but also with fear. And see, that's the thing about living after a loss. The good moments are good. They can be really good. But they'll always remind you of everything left you have to lose.

As I slide my butt onto one of the barstools at the counter, my father glances up to smile at me before turning back to the stove. The air's rich with the scent of garlic and heat, and my shoulders droop, my mind lulled with the rhythm of his movement and the promise of food. He stirs something in a saucepan, then splashes a hint of red wine in, followed by a sprinkle of parsley and white pepper.

Before long he's serving heaping bowls of pasta and we move to the dining room, sitting across from each other. My brain feels muddled, distant, and I stare through the divided glass window at the darkness outside then down at my meal. I know I should say something, that I should put voice to what I'm feeling and thinking, but don't have it in me to go over it all. To recount the events of this whole terrible cryptic day.

Where would I even begin?

26

After dinner, I help my dad wash up and put the dishes away. Then I kiss him good night and watch as he heads to his back office to do more work. He came home just for me, I realize, as I do some retreating of my own, hurrying up the stairs to lock myself in my room with Lemon in an effort to make sense of what's happening.

On a sheet of paper, I write:

IRIS MULVANEY—NOT MISSING, BUT NOT HERE.
*IN TROUBLE, PER YOUNGER BROTHER

SEACREST HOA—POWER HUNGRY, CHILDREN LOST, SURVEILLANCE?

CHRISSY'S BOYFRIEND A, WENT TO MIT, SCHOLARSHIP?

DEPUTY WILLIAMS???

CLUE: HAND, BRAIN, OATMEAL

THEN:
CARLOS DATED EDEN???

THEN ALSO:
LEIF . . . WHAT IS HE RUNNING FROM?

My eyelids grow heavy, but I keep going. I flip open my laptop and navigate to the folder where I've been keeping my research into the Chrissy Lambert case. It takes a second to sort through my collection of scanned news sources, but I find what I'm looking for—a pdf of an article from the *Central Cove Gazette* dated July 1986.

LAMBERT KILLING SPURS CITIZENS INTO ACTION

A group of local citizens are mobilizing to protect themselves and their families after the gruesome killing last year that took the life of Mayor Lambert's 17-year-old daughter, Chrissy.

"We're done cowering in our homes and wondering if we'll be next."

Mrs. Jacqueline Rosewood, 43, a close friend of the Lamberts, says she's been terrified ever since the murder and has resorted to self-defense training for her and her daughters. However, it's not enough, she says, which is why Mrs. Rosewood and 11 others showed up last Saturday at the first meeting of the Seacrest Neighborhood Crime Watch group. Cookies from Green Earth Bakery were served, and the group discussed action items such as a late-night escort program, a phone tree for reporting suspicious behavior, and firearms training.

"This is personal . . . These are our children."

Sheriff Tupper stated that he's pleased with the community engagement around safety, though he cautions residents against confronting anyone on their own. "That's what we're here for," he told the *Gazette*. Still the newly formed Neighborhood Watch members expressed concern over the sheriff's ability to protect Cabot Cove's most precious residents. "All of our daughters knew Chrissy—she was their friend—and to this day no one's been held accountable for her murder," said Mrs. Emily Wright. "How can we trust a system that's already failed to work? This is personal. These are our children."

This is personal.

I sit up. Stare at the accompanying photo of mothers and their teenage daughters gathered around a tray of catered cookies as a theory starts to form in my mind.

No way.

I open another file, one containing the guest list of Mayor Lambert's birthday party, and quickly cross-check the names listed in the newspaper photo. It's a perfect match. All six of the mother-daughter pairs in attendance at Jacqueline

Rosewood's self-defense training were at the party where Chrissy had died by suicide.

But here's what's even more notable: Among this group are the mothers—and grandmothers—of each missing teen.

Jax, Benson, Iris, and Trent.

27

THE FOLLOWING MORNING, I DITCH out on school. I don't bother asking Evie for help and I don't call in sick. I just head out first thing, leaving only a handwritten note for my dad telling him roughly where I'm going.

Traffic's light as I ride my bike over to the stone steps cut into the jagged hillside. Here, I hop off and make my way on foot to the place where this all started.

Meet me at the Hollow . . .

It took time to process, but I've absorbed enough about tenace and its rules to understand that yesterday's scarecrow wasn't just meant to scare and repulse me. No, thanks to the note card's red ink, it's also evident that those words were a directive.

So now I'm here.

But *why*?

Climbing the staircase at sunrise feels very different from that Friday evening almost a week ago. Cloudy skies mean the view's not as vast or as brilliant, but that doesn't keep my mind from spinning with vertigo from the height. My back's wet with sweat by the time I reach the top and enter the clearing.

I do a couple sweeps of the area, although I'm not sure what I'm looking for. Something. Anything, really, that will help me understand what happened that night. The cops said there were footprints—multiple—near where Jackson's phone and wallet were found, but it's hard to tell what's different. Plus, there are indications that more partying's gone on since I was last in the Hollow. I spot an empty case of PBR and subsequent empties scattered among the pine needles.

I keep searching. There's a discarded flannel, an old military blanket, a small pile of cigarette butts, a bottle of nail polish—black—and a few crumpled receipts. I pick these up and smooth them out. The first is from two days ago for a tank of gas and the case of beer from a local gas station that I recognize. Another, however, is older. From nearly three weeks ago, and it's from the computer and mobile phone repair shop in town. The services aren't itemized, but the total amount was for $234.56.

Shoving the receipts into my pocket, I do what I didn't that chilly Friday night—I climb into the treehouse. When I get inside, I don't find evidence of a party. Instead, there are a few rolled-up sleeping bags, a not-insignificant stash of canned food and bottled water, a camping stove, flashlight, and other gear, like matches and batteries.

I also spot a stray walkie-talkie—just one—and a worn paperback book titled *The Little Girl Who Lives Down the*

Lane. This sounds familiar and I pick it up. The book's ancient, published in the seventies, but reading the summary, I realize I know it. Or the movie version at least, with Jodie Foster. It was on a list of "10 Best Horror Movies Set in Maine Not Based on Anything Written by Stephen King," which I watched all of. This one was about a brilliant young girl who lives a secretive life with her father in small-town Maine, and she's perpetually tormented by nosy, judgmental—and ultimately predatory—neighbors.

But finding it here, I'm baffled.

What is going on?

I find a pair of binoculars, too. They're resting on an exposed beam running below one of the treehouse's few "windows," which is really just a narrow gap in the planks of wood. Pushing aside my concerns about germs and surface contaminants, I press the binoculars to my eyes and peer outside.

At first, I see nothing. Just a fuzzy blur of shadows. Reaching up, I twist the dial over the lenses until they focus. Everything is water. A vast expanse of waves and whitecaps. I pull the binoculars down until I hit land. Rocks at first—the entire Maine coast is littered with craggy outcrops and a few good-sized islands. Desert Island, near Bar Harbor, is even home to a vast national park and boasts the highest peak on the eastern coastline.

It's hard to get a sharp look at anything, however. The space between the planks is tight and not square, but the binoculars shift suddenly as I push forward and everything comes into view. No longer aimed at the water, I'm now looking down at the Northfield Marsh, which is a horseshoe-shaped wildlife preserve, consisting of intertwining networks of wooden bridges and walkways leading visitors through the shady foliage to view birds and frogs and snakes of all kinds.

I set the binoculars down. The view's undeniably gorgeous, but glancing around the treehouse again, I feel more unsettled than ever.

There're answers here. I'm sure of it.

Why don't I know the right questions to ask?

× × ×

My next stop is my great-aunt's north-side home. I don't know why, but when I arrive I stash my bike along the side of the house, where it's hidden from view. Am I protecting her?

Or me.

And from what?

Dr. Hazlitt's not around when I knock this time. It's a nurse I don't recognize, but she lets me in and tells me Aunt Jess is awake and finishing breakfast in the library. Heart pounding, my chest tight, I walk down the hallway and into that beautiful room, spacious, rich, and lined floor to ceiling with books.

"What's wrong, dear?" she asks as I settle on the brocade couch beside her.

"I need your help," I say. "I don't understand what's happening. Or why. All I know is that I'm in the middle of something, but I can't see where I am. It's like, maybe I'm in danger. Or maybe everything's my fault. Or maybe I'm close to figuring it all out. But I can't tell!"

"Is this about the boy that's missing?" she asks.

I nod.

"Tell me what you know," she says. "All of it."

28

HERE'S THE OTHER THING ABOUT secrets: There are some that absolutely need to be told.

At least, this was what Dr. Wingate had told me after I'd confessed my fears for Jackson's well-being. I was in eighth grade at the time, just shy of thirteen, and I could feel my friend slipping away from me. That what I'd always taken as our shared sense of cynicism and the backbone of our friendship had recently morphed into something darker.

Something I could no longer relate to.

"What's different?" Dr. Wingate asked. "Did anything happen recently that would explain this change in his behavior?"

What had changed? I thought about this. In a way, nothing had changed, but also, what *hadn't*? That was really the essence of it all. So many confused feelings between us and words left unspoken. We weren't children anymore and we never would be again. This thought had begun haunting me. The way time only takes you further from the people and places you love.

So what good was it?

Time was certainly no friend of Jackson's. He'd entered

the throes of puberty that year—a mild-mannered mouse of a boy suddenly sprouting into a full-throated teenager, with all the accompanying horrors. His voice had deepened. His muscles grew and any of his prior baby softness had melted away, lost to summer months of swimming and bike riding and collecting frogs. He'd also vacationed in Croatia—visiting the ancestral homeland from which the Glanvilles hailed.

When he returned from traveling and school started up again, I'd barely recognized him. We'd previously been united, he and I against the world, hiding from other students and sharing our most secret thoughts. I'd talk endlessly about death and anxiety and murder and how one day I hoped to solve a mystery big enough to change the world. Big enough, even, to ward off my own fear of death. Jackson also had a fondness for mystery, but the weirder kind. The mass vanishing at Roanoke. The deaths on Dyatlov Pass. Even that lake in Africa that killed thousands of people overnight by emitting a noxious gas.

But now, I told Dr. Wingate, he wasn't interested in anything.

"It's his parents," I finally said. "He's so consumed with making them happy. Doing what they want him to do and trying to do it before they even know what it is they want in the first place."

"What does that look like?" he asked.

"Playing basketball. Doing robotics. Joining the change ringing group at his church."

"And these are bad things?"

"Not on their own," I said. "But he's only doing them because they want him to. Because they'll make his life miserable if he doesn't live up to their standards."

"How would they make his life miserable?"

"He's terrified they'll send him to military school. Or worse."

"What's worse?"

I explained how Jackson had told me he'd found a brochure in his dad's office for a reform school out in Utah. One of those "troubled teen" programs that claimed free thinking and parental permissiveness were the literal products of Satan. Because apparently, if a child believed they had the power to choose their own path in life, then that meant truth was relative and God might as well not exist. This program ensured your child would be saved from such permissive indoctrination and learn to submit and therefore be healed from all sorts of problematic ailments: addiction, bad grades, bad attitude, mental illness, disobedience, immoral behavior, sinful thoughts. The list went on.

Dr. Wingate frowned at this description and asked if I knew the name of the program. But I'd forgotten.

"They watch him, you know. They put trackers on his phone and they have multiple cameras set up in that house. We found one in his room once," I said. "But you want to know what really worries me?"

"What's that?" he asked, and I told him about what Jackson had said about how part of him longed to jump from the North Minuet Bridge so that he'd never have to worry about being sent away or made to comply or disappointing the people who were never anything but disappointed in him in the first place. He said once the thought was in his head, he had no way of escaping it. He just kept replaying himself climbing over the bridge railing, rolling into the water below.

"I tried getting his mind off that by talking about things he's into," I said. "I asked him what mysteries he was researching. He'd been obsessed with that missing airplane thing. The Malaysian one. Also the human feet that keep washing up in British Columbia."

"Multiple feet? As in, more than two?"

"At least twenty at this point," I said.

"What was his answer?"

"He said he wasn't researching anything at the moment. That the plane had crashed, and the feet thing was easily explained. In fact, there *were* no more mysteries, he said. Everything had an answer and so there was no more reason for him to wonder."

"Wonder about what?"

"Anything," I said.

This was when Dr. Wingate had handed me the phone and told me the greatest gift I could offer my friend would be to take him seriously, to try and get him the help he so clearly needed.

So I did.

29

"BUT YOU MADE UP, THE two of you," my great-aunt says. "I thought he'd forgiven you and that he knew you'd done it out of love."

"We did make up," I tell her. "But what if something else was going on? Not just the stuff with his parents, but something else he was worried about but didn't feel safe enough to tell me? That he didn't feel safe telling anyone?"

"Like what?"

"I don't know exactly," I say. "But can I show you something that I found?"

"Of course."

I slide my laptop out of my backpack and power it on, quickly pulling up the old news article I'd reviewed the night before.

"You see here, the names of the people who started the original Seacrest Crime Watch group that eventually became the Seacrest Homeowners Association?"

Aunt Jess scans the screen. "Sure. Just who I'd expect to be involved in something like that. Cabot Cove society types."

"Right. That's what stood out to me, too. That here are the wealthiest families in town, and *they're* the ones claiming to be scared of crime. So scared that they bulldoze right over the sheriff's concerns and form their own vigilante group. One that today uses private security to patrol their neighborhood and enforce their wishes."

"I'm following."

"Now look at this." I pull up a second article. An earlier one from the night before Chrissy's body was discovered. It features photos from her father's elegant country club birthday party in the ballroom. The room's filled with glamorous families in beautiful clothes.

Aunt Jess squints a little and I try expanding the size of one photo in particular. It's a group shot—maybe a dozen or so mothers and daughters decked out in satin and taffeta and tons of hairspray. Conspicuously missing from the image are Chrissy and her mother.

"They're all the same people." I point. "I have the guest list for confirmation. They were *there* the night Chrissy died. They were probably the ones who found her in the women's bathroom in the first place, before her dad cooked up the golf course murder scene to keep her cause of death a secret. But all these people knew what really happened to her and they helped cover it up. And maybe they thought they were doing right by Chrissy's family. But they *knew* there was no murderer and yet they started this crime watch group anyway."

"What're you trying to say?" my great-aunt asks.

"The four kids who have gone missing—Trent, Iris, Benson, and Jackson. Their mothers were all there that night. Their grandmothers, too. They're in these photos."

"You're sure about this?"

"Yes. And they all currently live in Seacrest. Some of their last names are different because of marriage. But it's them."

Aunt Jess nods slowly, puts a finger to her lips. "Interesting. Very interesting. So you think that if all these present-day disappearances are connected, that the common link between them is—what? Being on the HOA board?"

"That's the link *now.* But I think they've shielded themselves behind the HOA based on something that happened then. Something having to do with Chrissy."

"Huh. How old was Chrissy when she died?"

"Seventeen. Around the same age as all four of the missing kids. And the same age their mothers were in these photos."

"What're you thinking?" Aunt Jess asks.

"That someone's targeting them for a reason. But who would do that?"

"I haven't the slightest idea who," she says. "But I have a suspicion that you might know *why.*"

"You do?"

She nods and right then, it clicks.

"I *do,*" I tell her.

30

BACK OUTSIDE. THE FIRST THING I do is text Leisl:

911

We need to meet.

We need to get into the whale head room.

She replies instantly.

I already have.

Hurry.

×××

I grab my bike and point it toward Broadmoor. But the day's unseasonably warm; I'm wearing jeans and a hoodie, and the school is nearly six miles away.

All uphill.

I start off slow and focus on keeping a steady pace and a sense of momentum. The first mile is relatively flat, thankfully. I'm cutting through town, rolling past the churches, the park, even the high school, where students are still stuck in their classrooms.

Another quarter mile gets me out of town and into the countryside. The foliage grows increasingly thick and vibrant as the climb grows increasingly grueling. Soon sweat soaks my clothes. My back aches and my thighs chafe. Adding insult to injury, hordes of sleek cyclists keep racing past me. It would appear Thursday afternoon is prime time for group leaf-peeping rides, and it's just one more thing that makes me doubt myself and my ability to finish what I've started, which is to bring Jackson home.

One way or another.

Pant.

Pedal.

Pant.

If Dr. Wingate were here, he'd tell me to *think positive* and to *set attainable and measurable goals.* But what happens when I'm positive that what's attainable for me won't get me up this mountain? Not in the near future, at least. I'm too slow. Too weak.

"Come on, Fletcher," I growl.

This is for Jackson.

This is for the Cabot Cove four.

I grit my teeth. Push harder.

You can do this.

A chorus of howling sirens suddenly fills the air behind me. Panicked, I flail and aim my bike at the road's shoulder before leaping off. Wheeling around, I crouch in the brush and watch as three full-size fire engines fly by, sirens blaring, horns honking, and lights flashing. They're soon followed by an ambulance. Then a cop car. Then another ambulance.

Heart pounding, I look all around, out over the hillside,

trying to determine what's going on. Then I smell it—acrid and sharp. Smoke. I peer up the mountain until I spot where it's coming from. A billowing black cloud spills out from what must be the south side of the Broadmoor property, directly below the castle. The trees are thick, still ripe with foliage, but even so, I make out what must be flames, licking and leaping for the sky.

"Holy *crap*," I breathe.

A new stream of cars whips past me, but when there's a break in the traffic, I hop back on my bike, shift to the lowest gear, and *push*.

×××

Almost there. The closer I get, the thicker the smoke grows. It burns my eyes, my lungs, but I keep going.

Rounding a final hairpin curve, I come out of the trees, and pass below an open arched gate that welcomes me to Broadmoor Academy. The scene greeting me in the main parking lot is total chaos. Emergency vehicles crowd the parking circle. The fire engines have their ladders out, equipment strewn everywhere, and firefighters run and shout commands while guiding hoses through the trees. Dark smoke clouds the air, and streams of water and foam flood the roadway.

To the north, students and staff have gathered on the upper lawn, watching the emergency unfold from a safe distance. Dumping my bike over a guardrail and shoving it into the bushes, I turn and scramble toward the crowd, swiping at my eyes and gasping for fresh air. Once I'm above the billowing smoke, I can finally see what's burning, and my heart drops. It's the library, Broadmoor's crown jewel.

More engines arrive, sirens screaming, and I turn to scan the crowd. Two ambulances are parked on the access road on the far side of the lawn, away from the fire. I walk toward them, eager to move even farther from the smoke. The ambulance closest to me has got its doors flung open, and as I approach, I can see someone sitting on the vehicle's back edge, bare legs dangling, and they've got an oxygen mask on.

An EMT steps back, giving me a clear view and my stomach knots. It's *Leisl*. I break into a run, watching as the EMT returns to place a foil blanket around her, and that's when I notice Leif standing to the side and arguing with a second EMT. His once-pretty face is clouded with fury, and he appears to be shouting. Carlos is there, too, I realize. He's kneeling beside Leisl, holding her hand, and the expression on his face is one of utter despair.

"What happened?" I say as I reach the back of the ambulance. "Are you okay?"

Leif's mouth drops open, like he's getting ready to yell at *me*. But before he can do that, Leisl rips her oxygen mask off, leaps up, and throws her arms around me.

"I'll tell you everything later," she whispers before Leif can pull her back. He shoves the oxygen mask back over her nose and mouth.

I watch Leif hover over his sister, then crouch beside Carlos. It's quieter down here, near the ground, and in a surreal haze, it feels as if we're sheltered from the panic and hysteria that's simmering above.

"Bea!" he exclaims. "How'd you get here?"

"I rode my bike. The fire—you can see it all the way from town. It's awful. I'm so sorry."

He nods.

"Is she okay?"

"She will be," he says, lowering his voice. "She was *there*."

I think quickly. "In the library?"

He nods. "Someone started it on purpose. Leisl caught him in the act. He tried to trap her in there. It could've been bad. But—" He cuts off, shakes his head.

"Who was it?" I ask and suddenly, I can scarcely breathe or think or move because it's him. I know it is. This proves my theory right. It also proves how desperate this situation is.

"Are you all right?" Carlos asks me.

I nod, holding my chest, trying to push down my panic.

"Just breathe," he says. "It's okay. Everything's going to be okay."

"I'm totally fine," Leisl announces, pulling the mask away again. "Leif's just making me sit here because he thinks that if he saves my life then I'll save his when he needs it."

"They said you had smoke inhalation," Leif snarls.

"Minor," she insists. "Minor smoke inhalation symptoms. Like when you smoke cloves."

One of the EMTs walks over and looks at the pulse oximeter on her finger. "Any trouble breathing, miss?"

She smiles. "None. The smoke smells bad, but my lungs don't hurt or anything."

"Can we get her away from here?" Carlos asks him. "Somewhere with fresh air?"

The EMT looks her over. "Your vitals are fine, so as long as you're willing to sign a waiver declining care, you can go. But check in with the school doctor later if you feel lightheaded or have any kind of pain."

Leisl gives him a thumbs-up and signs his form. "Sure thing."

"I'm submitting your medical record to the school, okay?"

"That's fine." She hops to her feet, shakes her hair, and gleams with golden-girl charm. "Thank you for saving me."

The EMT blushes. "Be careful, miss. You'll probably need to give a report to the police. Especially if this turns out to be arson."

"I will," she says as she waves and walks off. We follow after her like ducklings. Leisl makes a beeline for the arched walkway leading under the main building and toward the rear courtyard, where we're sheltered almost entirely from the fire and the chaos.

My head swivels as I walk. I've only been up here a few times in my life, and I forget how lush and old the place is. Everything is stone and green moss and classical lines. Leisl heads for a bench surrounded by ferns and ivy, and collapses onto it. Leif is there to catch her, and he murmurs something to her I can't hear and am not meant to. She turns to look at him and they're lost in some twin moment that's just for them.

Carlos takes my arm. "Let's leave them alone for a minute."

Together we walk farther into the winding campus, and I spy a few people peering out of windows from a row of small bungalow-type buildings.

"Who are they?" I ask.

"Faculty," he says. "Or more likely, their family members. A lot of teachers live up here. Some are in the dorms with students, but they also have housing for younger faculty who can't afford the real estate prices in town. The bungalows are tiny, but I think the school likes having families here. Makes it feel less cold. Or stern. Or something. You know, having kids running around."

"Sure," I say.

"They usually eat in the dining hall with us, so we get to know them pretty well."

"Do you like it here?" I ask.

He looks at me. "I like the science classes."

"That's right. What're you taking this year?"

"Atmospheric dynamics."

"I don't even know what that is," I say.

"You're not alone in that. But I came to Broadmoor specifically because of their atmospheric science department. It's pretty much one of a kind. We coordinate with one of the state universities and also a local company that's engaging in some high-end environmental research. We actually have access to their atmospheric laboratory."

"What do you do in an atmospheric laboratory?" I ask.

He grins. "Create weather."

"Wild," I say. Then, "Wait, what's the company?"

"Bio-Mar."

"Huh," I say.

Carlos stops, points through the trees. "You see it? The library? How there are four stories and then the roof's made of slate. It's gone now, though."

"The slate burned?"

"No. The roof collapsed when the cribbing holding it up caught fire."

"Oh."

"Anyway, Leisl can tell you what happened in more detail. But I guess she'd just gone into the library when the fire started. She says she saw someone slip out through the stairwell, and yelled for them to stop, but they didn't. And then she smelled smoke. So she pulled the fire alarm and tried to get out, only the stairwell door was locked."

"And Leif saved her?"

"Yeah, he came and was able to open the door from the outside."

"How did he know to do that?"

"She'd texted him. Good thing, too. It took the fire department more than ten minutes to get up here. They'll save the building, but my guess is everything inside is ruined."

"Aren't there sprinklers?"

"It's too old. Got grandfathered in."

"That's sad," I say.

"Yeah." He looks up at the smoldering structure. The fire's mostly out—the flames are gone, and what remains is once-clean mountain air that's now filled with the stench of charred wood.

The chilly reality of what's happened starts to sink in. Along with the implications. No one's supposed to know what Leisl and I have been looking into.

Yet someone does.

I lift my chin, vaguely aware that Carlos is looking at me. "Thank you for helping me earlier," I tell him.

"Panic attacks are the worst," he says.

I nod. "Think we should get back to them?"

"Sure thing," he says.

×××

Leisl looks even worse by the time we return. Her eyes are ringed red, her cheeks stained with tears. Leif, on the other hand, remains furious. At whom, I don't know.

Leisl pulls me to her, gripping me by the torso so tightly that I feel a little like a teddy bear she's afraid of losing. "Did Carlos tell you what happened?"

I nod.

"I couldn't do anything. I'm sorry. We'll have to find out who Chrissy's boyfriend was a different way."

I squirm out of her grasp. "But your text. You told me you'd gotten in."

"I *did*," she says. "I got the key and pulled all the yearbooks from that time period. But when I went to snap some photos, I realized I didn't have my phone. So I had to go all the way back to Madrone—that's my dorm—when you texted me, only it took me a while to get back because I'd reserved work time in the printmaking studio, like, over a week ago. I couldn't just ditch, and by the time I got to the library again . . ."

"It was on fire," I finish.

Leif glares at me, his face flush with rage. "You're telling me this is your fault? *You're* the reason she went in there?"

"I'm s-sorry," I stammer. "I'd just asked for help researching an old cold case. One of the people involved attended Broadmoor back in the eighties. We just wanted to know who he was and it made sense to look in the library. Neither of us thought anything like this would happen."

"His name starts with *A*," Leisl chirps brightly.

"A lot of names start with *A*," Carlos says.

But Leif isn't deterred. He takes a step toward me, jabbing his finger in accusation. "So it *is* your fault! My sister was doing you a favor and you nearly got her killed. How *dare* you pull her into something like that!"

"Don't be dramatic." Leisl grabs for his arm, pulls him back. "No one tried to kill me."

"That's literally what happened!" he screeches.

"He's right," I say. "I'm so sorry, Leisl. I had no idea. But this guy—whoever he is—he must've set that fire to stop us from figuring out who he is. I think he's the one who's responsible for everything that's been going on."

Leisl gapes. "*Everything?* You mean—"

"Yes. He's been living in that old treehouse at the Hollow. At least . . . I think so." I quickly explain about the photo at the country club, how it was taken the same night Chrissy had hanged herself. How a group of girls who were there agreed to lie about what had happened and then later grew into women willing to exploit any tragedy so long as it got them whatever special treatment they wanted. What they felt they deserved.

"So it's about *payback*?" she says. "This old boyfriend's mad at some women for lying about his girlfriend's death way back when?"

"Not just lying! For being part of the elitist group that rejected him! For making Chrissy feel as if her dreams and desires weren't good enough. It broke her. So maybe he's been planning this for years—waiting for Chrissy's supposed friends to grow up and then stealing their children so that they know what it's like."

"I'm sorry," Carlos interjects. "*Who* is this person?"

"We told you. We don't know his name," Leisl says. "But he went here, to our school, and he would've graduated in the eighties. A scholarship kid, we think. Oh, and he went to MIT."

"A killer from MIT," Carlos says. "I would not have guessed it."

"No one said *killer*," I snap because that's a possibility I'm not ready to face. "He could be holding them hostage. Demanding ransom."

"Mens et Manus," Leif grumbles.

My head snaps up. “What was that?”

“It’s the MIT motto.” He sneers at me. “What? You haven’t heard of it?”

I shake my head.

“‘Mind and Hand,’” he translates. “Guess I still know a couple of things you don’t.”

“How noble.” Carlos rolls his eyes, but now I’m looking at Leisl who’s looking back at me with a startled expression on her face.

Mind and hand, we’re both thinking.

And oatmeal?

31

THE FIREFIGHTING WINDS DOWN WITH the fire itself, and as hoses are rewound and ladders lowered, a loud bell echoes out across the school grounds. This is followed by a woman's voice blaring from a loudspeaker.

"Attention all Broadmoor students, staff, and faculty. We will be meeting in the all-school theater in fifteen minutes. This is a mandatory meeting. Attendance will be taken, and we will be extending the dinner hour until seven fifteen tonight to make up for the time this meeting will take. Thank you, see you soon, and remember to be Broadmoor strong."

"Who's that?" I ask.

"Headmistress," Leif says. "Broadmoor strong, my ass."

Carlos sighs. "They already took attendance. Like, they know nobody died. So what're they going to say? 'The library burned down. Please don't use the copier.'"

"I should get out of here," I say. "Leisl, I'm so glad you're all right. Maybe, call me later, if you feel up to it? Otherwise, I'll worry."

She smiles and hugs me, kissing my cheek. "I will."

I get up to go.

"Hold on," Leif says.

I lift an eyebrow.

"What were you doing here in the first place? If Leisl was going to find out who this guy was, why did you come?"

"Oh." I think fast. "Well, I was meeting Leisl at the library. I wanted to see the yearbooks for myself."

"Ah." He nods knowingly. "So it's possible we have this all wrong."

"What do you mean?"

"Maybe the guy Leisl saw in the library wasn't really after her. Maybe he was trying to kill you."

It takes me a beat to answer. "Yeah, Leif. Maybe he was."

×××

I grab my bike from the bushes, but my legs feel weak, drained. Was someone trying to kill *anyone*? Or was the fire merely a way of destroying evidence? All of it seems strange, since no one knew what we were doing, although when I think back on what I wrote in my last column, tracking down Chrissy's mysterious boyfriend might've seemed like the obvious next step.

So, in a way, maybe *everyone* knew.

I pull my phone out and check the comments on my latest column, quickly scanning over a lot of the expected bickering and searching for the name I'm interested in.

There he is.

theuncouthswain.

We need to meet, he writes. It's urgent.

A cool rush of dread washes over me. I look around. This comment was only posted ten minutes ago, and once again, it feels as if the author might know where I am. As if they might be able to see me.

The parking lot crowd's thinned significantly. The only vehicles left include a news truck, a single cop car, and an ambulance. People are milling around the burned library and someone's taking photographs of the site, but the Broadmoor students have retreated to their all-school meeting in whatever auditorium they do that sort of thing.

I walk over to the library and observe the fire's aftermath. An ache of sadness builds in my chest, imagining all that's been lost. Not just history and documents, but moments. Memories, stretched across generations and shared by thousands—all gone.

"Beatrice." I whirl around. The sun's dipped behind the mountains already, a cool autumn moon is on the rise, and the person speaking to me is none other than Deputy Williams.

"What're you doing here?" he asks, hands on his hips.

"What are *you* doing here?"

"There was a fire," he says. "In case you hadn't noticed."

"I was visiting a friend," I tell him. "Or . . . I was supposed to. Is it true it was arson?"

"Who told you that?"

I hedge my response. "Some of the students."

"Which ones?"

I don't answer.

"Never mind," he says. "But you shouldn't be here. You know that, right?"

"No," I say. "I don't know that. In fact, you're the one who told me to look into things, and that's what I'm trying to do."

He frowns. "I didn't tell you to look into *this*."

"What is this?" I ask.

He doesn't answer.

"Fine." I turn and walk away, returning to my bike. I pull my helmet on and curse myself for postponing my departure. It's near dark now and the thought of riding the twisty roads is not only unappealing.

It's terrifying.

I'm not totally unprepared. I switch on the flashing red light attached to the rear of the bike as well as the white light I've got mounted on the front, in the center of the handlebars, above the gearshifts. Then I shove off, front wheel wobbling at first before steadying. Riding the brakes on the steep sections, I endeavor to stay as close to the edge as possible, but it's more frightening this way.

For most of the descent, I'm on the cliff side, and a sharp wind's kicked up. It buffets me from the back, straining to blow the bike out from under me and toss me to the ground. I also can't hear anything, and more than once I'm startled by oncoming vehicles, swooping by with the high beams on to momentarily blind me. More and more people are heading up to campus, it seems, now that the fire's out.

Like moths to a flame, it's human nature to gawk at tragedy. Although it's not like I'm any better. Isn't that what true crime is? Society of the spectacle?

My palms ache from gripping the bars. Tape's long

frayed and blisters have begun building up at the base of my fingers. A waning moon rides high, teasing me through the trees, through forest gloom.

Two more miles. I pedal faster, start to take the turns tighter. Whatever I can do to get off this mountain.

Then suddenly I feel it. A cool lick of fear breathing down the back of my neck. It's not the wind, and I risk a glance behind me only to go weak with terror at what I see: There's a car riding tight on my butt and its headlights are off.

I correct right, almost too far, and send myself hurtling toward the cliff before straightening out at the last moment. I'm riding right on the edge, just blackness below, and I'm waving the car past, telling it to pass.

Only it doesn't.

I wave again. It's so dark and I've got no way to tell this driver that their lights are off. But as I slow, they slow, the sedan's front bumper jolting dangerously close to my rear tire. But not hitting it. Whoever's behind the wheel is comfortable waiting me out, nudging me down this mountain and into what? Another trap like the burning library? But one I can't escape?

No way. I grit my teeth, lower my chest to the bars, and push hard. My legs spin furiously as I drop the gear, praying that my janky chain will stay on. I hear it clunk and shift and slide into place, making the transition so that my turns have power. Losing this car won't be easy, but the alternative's a lot harder.

My sudden sprint takes the driver by surprise, and I pull

out in front, racing for the downhills, racing for safety. The car honks in surprise and accelerates, pulling up behind me and revving its engine to express its displeasure. The car then zigzags across the road, brakes burning and squealing.

Crap. This driver has a serious death wish. I ride faster, as fast as I can. Just a half mile more. I can make it.

At the base of the hill is a roundabout with four outlets. Keeping straight will take me into town. To the right will carry me into a residential area, one with tight winding streets and a maze of courts and cul-de-sacs. To the left will lead me into the marshlands. The ones I saw through the binoculars.

Whizzing down asphalt, I have a split second to make my move. I sense the car slowing to watch where I go, and as I enter the roundabout, I switch my headlight off. There's nothing I can do about the red one on the back, but I'm hoping it won't matter. I race the roundabout as the car falters, trying to pick up where I've gone. It edges into the roundabout, waiting for confirmation as I circle back past the middle point and turn uphill toward the marshlands outlet.

In response, the car eases forward a little more, edging past the first outlet, and this is when I commit—flying all the way around the roundabout again and coming up *behind* the car.

The vehicle—it's a gold Nissan—stops short, realizing it's lost me. I bide my time on their back bumper, breathing in the idling exhaust fumes. The car crawls forward again, and I try and get a look at who the driver is. In the darkness, all

I see is the outline of thin hands on the wheel. And then I'm gone, flying into the residential foothills, unsure if there's even a route that will lead me out or if I'm riding into a dead end.

In a way it doesn't matter. Behind me I hear the screech of the car reversing back up the roundabout and turning down the street after me. What does matter is that I'm winning. That I'm still ahead.

For now.

32

I CURSE MYSELF AND MY choices almost immediately. The first street I turn down is indeed a dead end. I have to wheel around, double back, and continue on the main road. The second street curves around and around until I end up bisecting the original one and nearly run right into the Nissan. Reaching to switch on my headlight again, the beam shines right into the driver's seat. I strain for a better look, but whoever it is throws an arm up, turns their head.

Furious, I pedal farther on the main road, passing newer housing developments, ones built into the hillside to take advantage of the view. I have the upper hand in my ability to move around, there just isn't anywhere to go. This is a slow-motion foxhunt destined to end like all others. Unless . . .

Up ahead is the bougie Birch Hills housing development. It's no Seacrest, but it boasts newish five-bedroom homes on lush lots and a community pool and gym. The development's built on a dead-end road so I don't dare ride up there. Instead, I throw my bike down on the sidewalk and head out on foot. I turn down an eastern-facing street, only to crouch in the driveway of the second house I come across. As I wait for the Nissan to creep past, I hold my breath and hope a motion-sensored floodlight doesn't come on.

The sedan rolls slowly down the street, exhaust puffing into the wet night air, and when I can't hear it anymore, I crawl on hands and knees along the side of the house and slip into the backyard. Here I look around cautiously. There are lights on in the kitchen and on the second story, but the yard's empty save for a small cat sleeping in a planter box. I scratch her ears and keep moving. Hopping the back fence is terrifying, but no one shoots me, no dogs attack, and there's no sign of the car on the other side.

I scramble across the street, all hunched over like a werewolf or an anteater, and make my way up the steep drive to Birch Hills Circle. Here, eight stately homes ring a wide paved cul-de-sac, and I don't hesitate or worry about floodlights anymore. I run straight for the one house I know and pound on the front door. Ring the bell. Repeat.

Hurry up, I think. *I know you're in there.*

With a shiver and gasp, I risk a glance down the street. Is that an engine I hear? Purring in the distance? My heart lurches, and I pound the door again.

The porch light comes on.

Another glance—I can see the headlights now, only the car's not approaching. It's just idling at the end of the block, like it's waiting for something.

Then again, maybe it's not.

It strikes me then that I've likely gotten this whole thing wrong. That this car never intended to catch me. It wanted me to run. Just like I did and just like it knew I would. Just like a lost sheep that's been herded right back to its swain.

33

THE FRONT DOOR OPENS.

It's Dr. Wingate. He stands in the foyer of his large home wearing a thick, chunky gray sweater and dark corduroy pants, and he's staring at me standing sweaty and gasping on his porch on a Thursday night.

"Bea?" he says. "Are you all right? Come in."

I step into the foyer on shaky legs. I've been coming here for nearly five years, and I've never entered this part of the house. Dr. Wingate's office is in a separate in-law space on the floor below and I've always accessed that by going through the yard, past the koi pond.

Of course, I've often fantasized about his real life, what it might look and feel like and how he chooses to live. It's the most unfair thing about therapists or psychiatrists—that the relationship only goes one way. They get to learn everything about you while concealing their own emotional landscape because professionalism is just another word for secrecy. But now, walking into his house, even in my panicky haze, I can't help but absorb the tiny details. The wood floors and bronze sculptures of horses displayed on floating shelves. The rustic wall sconces and classical music streaming from hidden speakers. The rich scent of food, something comforting and full of spice on a cold night.

"Sit down." He leads me into the living room through an arched doorway. The walls are lined with books, mostly science and politically themed titles, and a fire crackles in a stone hearth. "You look terrified. Were you in an accident?"

Was I? I turn and peer through the wide plate glass window looking out over the neighborhood. I spy house lights, trees, a tiny sliver of street.

The car's gone.

I straighten up again.

"Alex," a voice calls out. "Who was at the door?"

"I've got it," he calls back. "Come on, Bea. Sit. Get warm. You're shivering. Are you hurt anywhere?"

I stare at his sofa—at the beautiful brown leather upholstery, then down at my clothes. They're *filthy.* Not only torn and sweat soaked, but I'm smeared head to toe with what must be soot and smoke.

"Who's Alex?" I ask. "I thought your name was William."

"My name is William. Alex is my middle name. It's what my friends call me." He smiles. "Willy Wingate sounds a lot sillier than I am."

"Huh," I say.

"What happened to you?" he asks.

"There was a fire," I blurt out. "At Broadmoor. That's what happened. That's why I look like this."

"A fire?"

A short, strikingly beautiful woman who must be Dr.

Wingate's wife enters the room. She's far more stylish than he is; dressed in a long linen skirt and white asymmetrical top.

"Alex?" she asks.

"There's been a fire," he tells her. "Up at the boarding school."

"A bad one?"

"Burned down the library," I say.

"That's awful." She turns to her husband. "You should call Don. See if they need anything. See if the kids are okay."

Dr. Wingate nods. "I'll do that."

The woman comes toward me. She has dark hair, dark eyes, and even without makeup, she's got the smoothest skin I've ever seen. "I'm Alex's wife, Leah. I don't think we've met before."

"I'm Beatrice," I tell her. "I'm a patient. So sorry for interrupting—"

"You have nothing to be sorry for," she assures me, reaching for my hand, a row of silver bracelets jingling softly against her wrist. "Why don't we go upstairs while he makes that call. You can wash up, change your clothes. Then we'll eat. Okay?"

I stare at her as if in a dream. "Okay."

34

TWENTY MINUTES LATER, I'M UPSTAIRS in a tidy guest room, both freshly showered and freshly dressed in a pair of Leah Wingate's sweatpants and a soft fleece sweatshirt.

"Looks like we're the same size," she says brightly after knocking and coming in at my request. "I brought you these."

I take the thick pair of socks she's handed me and sit on the bed to pull them on. "Thank you. You didn't have to do all this."

"It's a bribe," she tells me as she gathers up my filthy clothes in a plastic bag.

"I'm sorry?"

"I want to hear about this fire. I'm hoping you'll tell me in exchange for food and clean clothes."

"Of course."

"Let's go down to the kitchen, then." She waves for me to follow. "Alex should be off the phone soon. He'll be heartbroken, you know. He has such fond memories of that campus."

I trail after this woman, this warm motherly woman, placing one hand on the wooden banister as we descend the staircase back to the first floor and enter a gleaming chef's kitchen with marble countertops and soft recessed lighting. She motions for me to sit at a large island and begins fixing a plate of roast chicken and vegetables.

"So does he work at Broadmoor?" I ask. "Or did he used to? Is that how he knows the library?"

"He's consulted with them in the past. They don't have a permanent mental health professional on staff, which they should. But he takes referrals, and in emergency situations, he's gone up there to work with students or assess a crisis concern." She turns back to look at me. "But no, his emotional connection to Broadmoor is from when he attended."

"He *went* there?"

"Indeed."

"I thought he was from California."

"That's right!" She places the food in front of me, which smells amazing. "He grew up outside of Bakersfield. In the valley, with all that heat and dust and deadly spores. It's a terrible and fascinating place. From a scientific perspective."

"Deadly spores?"

"Valley fever," she explains. "It's caused clusters of illness in the area, and it can be deadly. But I'm a pulmonologist so anything that causes respiratory illness is of particular interest to me. It's not a virus, though. It's a fungus."

"And after Broadmoor, he went to Dartmouth, right?" I ask. That's the diploma that hangs in his office. Although he's told me he did his residency in San Francisco. Maybe he wanted to get back to California but ended up here, in the place where he went to high school.

"He went to Geisel, yes," Leah opens the fridge and pours me a glass of sparkling water while I wolf down the chicken. "That's the Dartmouth School of Medicine, where he did a dual MD and PhD. Typical overachiever. But before that he was an undergrad in Boston."

"Boston?"

"Cambridge, really."

"This is delicious." I point to the food. Then, "So he went to Harvard?"

She laughs. "He wishes. Alex studied at a little nothing place called MIT."

I stare at her, absorbing what she's just said, as Dr. Wingate walks in. His face is grim, distressed. Weary, maybe, too.

"Library's a total loss," he announces. "I should probably get up there."

"What happened?" Leah asks.

"Don says the sheriff believes the fire was intentionally set. By whom, I don't know. I'm sure a thorough investigation will be done. But what a *waste*. That building was a historical site on its own, never mind the contents. It was the oldest building on campus. The stained glass was priceless." He pushes his hair back, straightens his glasses, then peers at me. "Do you need a ride home?"

I glance up at him, this man who's been a part of my life for such a long time. Who's seen me through my mother's death, my guilt over having Jackson committed, my own fears and anxieties about who I am and the world I'm living in. This man I've trusted with *everything*.

Until now.

"Bea?" he says, and that's when I remember seeing him at Jackson's vigil. How he stood alone on that boulder, gazing out to sea. I had thought he was there for me.

Now I don't know what to think.

"No, thanks." I slide off the chair I've been sitting in. "But hey, can I ask you something? It's related to what we were just talking about."

"Sure," he says.

"Is there any connection that you know of between MIT and oats? Or oatmeal?"

From the other side of the kitchen, Leah smiles widely. "She knows you well, Alex."

"What do I know?" I ask.

"All his pet interests. Like the Quaker Oats scandal." Seeing my confused expression, Leah continues. "In the forties, Quaker and MIT conducted a series of unethical food experiments on children who were wards of the state of Massachusetts. The researchers purposely misled a group of boys at the Fernald State Home into joining a special 'science club,' where they were fed irradiated oatmeal."

Startled, I glance up at Dr. Wingate. "That's your pet interest?"

"In a way," he says gruffly. "But I'm sorry, I don't have time tonight to unearth old tragedies like the Fernald science club. There are new ones afoot, and I really have to go."

× × ×

The ride home is almost unnervingly anticlimactic. I'm not followed or chased, nor do I do any following. Everywhere I look, I spy glowing pumpkins and other festive decorations. The smell of wood smoke is in the air, both remnants of the Broadmoor fire and the way hearty Mainers heat their homes on cold nights.

Once inside, I find our own living room equally homey and warm. Especially since my dad and uncle and some of their friends are seated around the dining room table for their monthly DnD game. They've been playing it for years, which is something I love. I used to sit and watch when I was younger, my anxious mind soothed by the stories they told and conflicts they encountered, always searching for anything I recognized from the real world. When I did, it felt like unearthing a gem, something rare and glittering and *true*. Like my father's grief. My uncle's loneliness.

Tonight, however, I just kiss them both, greet the others, and offer a brief recounting of the day, the fire, which they've all heard about. Then I walk upstairs, pull my door shut, and get online. I navigate to my column, to the comments, to theuncouthswain.

We need to meet, he'd written.

I'm not positive who he is, but I have a feeling in my bones. One strong enough to take a chance on replying.

Where?

Not five minutes go by before he responds and confirms my suspicions.

the secret garden

What time?

Sunrise.

35

IT'S STILL DARK WHEN I get there. I ride my bike through the fading late-night gloom all the way to the high school bike racks, where I lock it up. Then I walk back through Hillcrest Park until I reach the spot that's ours.

And only ours.

You can't see it from the street, but running between an art supply shop and a pet day care, there's this hidden path that leads from Cabot Cove's boutiquey shopping district up toward the more industrial part of town. Hanging plants and murals adorn the alleyway—mostly images of sea life and lobsters and ships struggling against the elements, although recent additions by the local art empowerment group are more diverse and more modern. Vibrant and alive, the alley's long been a common shortcut for students to use between classes or at lunch, when we're allowed to leave campus.

What's used less frequently, however, is the continuing stretch of this semi-urban walkway that winds away from Cabot Cove High, still avoiding the street by skirting past a consignment store, an auto shop, and finally snaking behind the Five Stars Brewery out to the entrance of Northfield Marsh, where the alley eventually ends.

No murals are painted on these walls, although any open spot's been covered in graffiti at some point in the recent past. The scent of piss is common, as is the sight of trash and worse, all thanks to the brewery. But if you walk to the very north end of the path, you'll find the most unexpected surprise—a hidden garden. You have to know where to look, tucked tight between the driveway and the dumpsters, but when you slip into it, it's like being inside an atrium. The walls are painted with bright swirling colors highlighting a singular image of a phoenix, wings outstretched as it takes flight above flames. Gorgeous shade plants abound—perched on the windowsill, the ground, a narrow ledge. I've never known who put these plants here or why or how they're cared for. There's also a tin plate of dry cat food that's left every day and a ceramic bowl filled with fresh water, although the plate's still empty this early and there's no sign of the neighborhood strays.

But this spot is where I know to wait. It's the garden I found on the day my mother died, a day I'd chosen to attend school despite knowing the end was near because the burden of waiting had grown so heavy. Hospice care had arrived, and the inside of our home felt like a bomb waiting to go off. Sometimes I imagined I could actually hear the countdown, that incessant *tick-tick-tick* inching toward a detonation my dad and I had both come to fear and secretly longed for.

It was a beautiful day, the day she died. Blue sky, warm air, and the scent of jasmine filling my nostrils as I walked the streets of Cabot Cove. I'd just gotten out of school—sixth grade—and, restless and agitated, I wandered the town, searching for a secret or a sign, a clue that my mother's suffering wasn't in vain, that her existence truly mattered and that some part of her would always remain here, on earth, never to be forgotten.

I'd followed the painted alley like I was following bread crumbs and somehow amid the stench and trash, I caught sight of the unmarked cutout in the wall. I slipped inside and saw the plants and cat food and the phoenix, and then I just stood there, frozen, for what felt like hours, staring out the small street-facing window, watching cars and people go about their day.

By the time I got home, she was gone.

But this spot is also where Jackson and I took to meeting last year once the snow had melted and our friendship was reborn. It's where we'd conspire, before and after school, planning for him to meet with Dr. Wingate. Planning a safety net so that he could be saved from his parents, who had failed him in every way possible and seemed determined to keep failing him.

And now I'm here again.

Alone.

But *why*?

The darkness is creepy. Mice are squeaking by the trash. But I stand and wait, and before long, the garden begins to brighten, lit by a warming orange sky spilling through the narrow street-facing window.

Sunrise.

A car horn beeps. In the predawn haze, I peer out and spot a car idling in the street. A gold Nissan sedan.

The old sheep dog's here, my mind whispers, *ready to return me to the flock*.

The driver honks again, then seems to turn toward me and lift a hand.

I exhale deeply, as a flutter of doubt awakens inside my core.

This is it, isn't it?

36

I REACH THE CAR AND open the passenger side door. With the engine running, this activates a soft chiming alarm, and it also turns on the overhead light, illuminating the driver. Iris Mulvaney.

I recognize her right away. Her once-dark hair's been bleached and cut short, but her features are distinctive—she's got a dimpled nose, round freckled cheeks, and a tight-lipped smile.

"What are you waiting for?" she asks. "Get in already."

"Do I have a choice?"

"Of course you have a choice. You're here, aren't you?" She holds out a hand. "Come on. I need your phone."

I get in and give it to her.

"Close the door. That sound's driving me nuts." Iris fusses with the back of my phone but manages to open it up and pull out the battery, which she swiftly locks in the glove compartment. "Don't worry. You'll get it back."

I close the door. Pull my seat belt on. "I saw your brother the other day."

She snorts. "You think I don't know that?"

"How did he know we were coming? Or should I ask how did you know?"

"Put this on." Iris hands me a sleeping mask. A silk one made with leopard-print fabric.

"Why?" I stare at the mask in bewilderment.

"Are we playing the Obvious Game? It's a blindfold. Put it on. We're going somewhere."

"Who's the uncouth swain?" I ask.

Iris sighs. Taps her black-painted nails on the steering wheel. "I don't have all day."

"And what was with that scarecrow?"

Now she laughs. "You liked that, huh? Lot of good it did you, though."

"I went to the Hollow."

"You could've gone other places, too, you know. Everyone's always saying you're so smart, only I don't see it. But hey, that's what I'm here for." She snaps her fingers. "Let's *go*, Fletcher. Put on the mask already. I don't make the rules."

I slide the blindfold on.

× × ×

The ride's a long one. At first, I try and orient myself to the map inside my head, wanting to reassure myself that my guess is correct and that I'm still somewhat in control of this situation. But it's an impossible task. Too many turns and lane shifts. Plus, Iris stops for gas at some point and manages to get stuck in traffic, which is quite a feat in rural Maine. The radio's no help either because she's listening to a podcast. Full irony alert: It's the same one I've been listening to, where each episode is narrated by a different character trapped on a ship. It's only now, however, that I finally understand that the ship they're on is traveling through space, not on the ocean, and that every passenger aboard has been convicted of a crime.

That they're all guilty.

But the ride stretches on and on, and eventually I do what I always do in cars—I sleep. But it's that fitful, pained sort of sleep that comes when you're overtired to start with and also it's daytime and you've been semi-kidnapped and the sun is beaming through the car window and your arm skin's roasting like a pig on a spit.

That kind of sleep.

We're heading north, my brain whispers in response to the skin-roasting observation, but then my head nods and drops and I'm in dreamland.

×××

In my dream that's maybe also a memory, I'm back on Jackson's grandfather's farm, and Jax and I are playing in the sunlit meadow while glossy, shivery-skinned horses graze and stamp the ground and swish their tails, this way and that. We're playing together in that way young children do when there's no difference between the sexes or our skin color. I mean, obviously there *are* differences in how we have and will be allowed to move through our worlds. But in this moment, in the ways we size each other up and assess our own abilities, we may as well be one. There's no doubt between us, no space separating our bond. We even grieve together as we mourn different sorrows. And our time here in this beautiful place, the one dotted with horses who breed and make babies destined to fly down racetracks to win ribbons and break legs, has likewise been coated with loss. It's not the place or the horses, though, but the people. Jackson's grandfather isn't a happy person, and Jackson's father isn't here, but he's not either. Happy, that is.

So what does that make Jackson?

I've lived this dream so many times that I know what's next—I'm distracted by a stranger entering the barn. Or what looks like a stranger. I can barely make out their shape. More like a shadow. Or an omen. But this time, Jackson tackles me and sends me to the ground.

I lie, stunned, watching upside down as he rises. Calls out to the person he sees.

It's not him, I try and gasp.

That's not your grandfather.

Someone else walks among us.

A stranger.

Or is it?

37

"WAKE UP," IRIS GROWLS. "WE'RE here."

I sit up, shove the sleep mask off, then look over at her. "Where?"

"You haven't figured it out yet? Hey, if not, welcome to paradise."

I blink and look around. The sun's high in the sky and the car we're riding in's surrounded by color. Pure autumn joy. Everywhere, the trees are ablaze, lighting the skyline with leafy flickers of bronze, rust, and gold. The road's paved but bumpy with neglect. On either side are wide green fields dotted with horses, thoroughbreds. I spy a pond. Then another. All ringed with more trees and no doubt ripe with turtles, snakes, and full-throated bullfrogs. Soon we pass a riding arena filled with jumps and poles on the ground for training. Up ahead is a hilly dip and beyond that I know exactly what I'll see.

Of *course*.

The car rises and drops, clattering along the road, and suddenly before us stretches the tree-lined valley of my dream. Iris slows and pulls up a gravel driveway to the main house, a long rambling Colonial with green shutters and peeling white paint. And beyond the house, I spot the barn. No longer detached from its stone foundation, however, it stands tall and strong against the clear blue sky.

Iris parks the car and we both step out, my mind tumbling with the implications of where we are and how my dream ties into it all. But everything's connected, I realize. It's always been this way. The past, the present, all the truths I've been chasing, they're knotted up as tight as the muscles in my back from that rattling car ride. I can barely stand. With a groan, I reach and place one hand on the Nissan's warm hood before stretching, arching, twisting my spine until it cracks, and right then the front door to the house opens, and someone wearing a red North Face jacket steps onto the sagging porch.

I straighten up and look right into Jackson's clear blue eyes.

×××

Fury. Fear. Misery. Resentment. *Joy*. I'm a storm cloud of emotions, but none strong enough to stop me from bounding toward my friend and wrapping my arms around him. I barely reach his chest, of course, but Jax bends down and pulls me to him.

"Oh, Bea," he says. "Can you ever forgive me?"

"What am I forgiving you for?" I ask, which is when I realize we're both crying.

He wipes his eyes, and motions for me to sit beside him on the porch step. I do and I take him in. It's only been a week and though he's still tall and muscular, with his warm smile and thick curly hair, there's something different in his mannerisms, in the way he holds himself.

He's relaxed, I realize. For the first time in what feels like forever, Jackson physically looks like he's at peace.

He reaches to take my hand, almost like he wants to make sure that I'm real, and I can feel how he's trembling, how nervous he is.

"I committed the perfect crime," he finally says. "My own kidnapping. You would have been so proud of me, Bea. You could've written a whole book about how careful I was."

"Could have?" I ask.

He nods, smiling through his tears. "It's all over now. I've brought in a witness to confess my sins to. Isn't that a violation of criminal rule number one?"

I laugh in spite of myself. "Tell no one."

"That's right."

"So why are you? If you wanted to run away and start a new life, why are you telling me? Why'd you bring me here?"

"I had to," he says. "I couldn't let you suffer any longer, wondering about where I'd gone or what had happened or if you were somehow responsible. That was the last thing I wanted."

"But that was the plan, wasn't it? It had to be."

"*No.* Not exactly. Some of it, sure. I always planned to leave, and I always knew you'd look for me. That *was* part of the plan. But I thought—well, I didn't know you'd take it so personally." His cheeks redden. "Or maybe I did, and I just convinced myself otherwise because I'm a coward. I'm sorry for that. You've always been so strong, Bea. Stronger than I am."

"I think you're very strong," I tell him.

He shakes his head.

"But why leave the way you did?" I ask. "The police and your parents are looking for you. You're a missing person. At the very least, you're a runaway. Why now? You've got enough credits to graduate early. You probably only had a year or so left and you would've been free to go."

"I didn't have a year," he says. "Not mentally, at least. I was in a bad place, Bea. Really bad. I felt trapped. And the cops weren't in any position to go up against my family."

I squeeze his hand. "I'm sorry."

Jackson sighs, then suddenly hops to his feet, wipes his hands on his jeans. "You remember this place, don't you? We came here when we were kids."

"Of course I remember it." Internally, I curse myself for not thinking to search here. But it hadn't crossed my mind, not even after the scarecrow's fake bomb clue that I'd failed to pick up on. Why was that? "In fact, I dream about this place all the time."

"You do?" He seems surprised at this revelation. "Weird."

"Your grandfather hit you here. In that barn."

His jaw tightens. "Yeah."

"Is that the place where he, you know, did what he did?"

"Built bombs and IEDs?" he asks. "And plotted to murder people?"

"Yeah, that."

"It sure was. There was a whole underground bunker down there. And that day when the bee stung you, I went in there. Saw everything. Well, I didn't understand what I saw at the time, but that didn't matter."

"Because he hit you."

"He hit me, he said, because he didn't want me getting hurt and that if I felt pain, then that was good a thing because it meant I was capable of learning right from wrong." Jackson smiles sickly. "The men in my family have a funny way of showing their love."

"That's not love."

"It's what he had to give."

"That was the day I vowed to keep you safe," I tell him.

He touches my cheek. "I made the same vow to you once. When we were kids."

"And you've kept it," I say. "I've never forgotten that."

Jackson gestures to the fields before us. "You know, I own this now. This place. The farm."

This is a surprise. "You *own* it?"

He nods.

"How?"

"That's a long story. The short version is that having a place of my own will greatly help my future emancipation case."

"I've got time for the long version," I offer.

"I'm sure you do."

"Does it involve *him*?" I ask, and suddenly I'm trembling, too. Broaching this topic can only deflate the magic of being with Jax, of knowing he's alive and seemingly doing well. Obviously, I would've given anything for this outcome, but I also know deals with the devil are often struck when survival is at stake. And I'm not sure Jax appreciates the danger he could be in—the danger we *both* could be in—if the person he's put his trust in turns out to be as monstrous as I fear.

But Jackson just pushes his hair back. Squints into the sun. "Hey, you want to go for a walk?"

I swallow the lump in my throat. I don't know where to go with this conversation. "Okay."

"Come." Once again, he takes my hand in his, his flesh so warm and real, and together we walk around the back of the house and step into a sunlit field bursting with the scent of warm hay, the promise of cool nights, and the rocketing passage of time. Horses whinny as we pass, and one even charges the pasture fence, stopping short only to toss its blazed head and half rear before galloping off in a cloud of dust.

We keep walking, circling the back pond, and it's as if we're traveling back in time with each step we take, returning us to who we were then, even if then we didn't know that any of this would matter.

Soon we're standing in front of the barn, no longer swaying, but it continues to loom large, leaving me dizzy as I strain to look at it.

"Is the bunker still there?" I ask.

He nods. "The feds took everything, obviously. As evidence. But yeah, it's still there."

"Have you ever gone in?"

Jackson drops my hand, puts his own to his chest and rubs there, hard, like something deep inside of him hurts. "Out of my formative male role models, one turned out to be a serial killer and the other uses sin as an excuse to punish me for any joy or pride I find in anything. It's made it hard for me to find purpose in life. In myself even. Because a question used to haunt me. One I used to ask myself every night before I went to sleep."

"What was that?" I ask.

He smiles weakly. "Are monsters born or made?"

38

As we continue a tour of the farm's wooded acres, we talk for at least an hour or so, mostly about the intricacies of Jackson's plan and my amazement at all the clues he left behind that I failed to pick up on. All the reasons he did what he did.

And for *whom*.

It's clear that out here he doesn't think he's in any danger from the Seacrest HOA or Chrissy Lambert's vengeful boyfriend or even his own parents, and I want to believe he's right. I want to believe everything he's telling me and trust that his truth is real because being with Jackson leaves my heart full, restoring a sense of rightness and awe in the fact that we've walked beside each other for so long and endured so much. We're heading back toward the main house when I hear the soft chug of an engine. I look up to see a gleaming black SUV gliding down the two-lane road.

My muscles tense. I can't help it. "It's him, isn't it?"

Jackson's eyes twinkle. "I see you've figured some things out."

"Jax, I don't think you understand. He could be—"

"I understand all that I need to," he says firmly. "Okay?"

I nod, frustrated. I need to approach this differently. "So, uh, what's Iris doing here?"

"Same as me. Planning the rest of her life."

"But her brother," I say. "He thinks she's coming back."

"Yeah. That's complicated. A lot of the abuse she endured is because she's Perry's half sister. Her mom remarried and they had him, but her stepfather hates her. Resents that she's not his, I guess, and her mom wants him to be happy."

"She was the one who was staying in the treehouse, wasn't she?"

"Yeah. I ran into her out there about a month ago. She'd been living there on and off for a while, and she told me I wasn't the only one who was being watched by Seacrest security. And followed. And tracked like an animal. She filled me in on a lot. Stuff I'd long suspected but didn't realize other people were experiencing, too. But that girl's a survivor. It took a while to get her to come out here. She doesn't really trust people."

"And that night in the woods?" I ask. "When we were supposed to meet?"

He nods. "That was us. Me and Iris. We had walkie-talkies that we'd bought in order to stage my so-called 'abduction.' I didn't mean to scare you as much as we did. Iris, uh, kind of likes being in character."

I scowl. "What about Benson and Trent?"

"As far as we know they're still in Utah at the troubled

teens program. The same one I would've been sent to if I hadn't gotten out when I did."

"You know this for a fact? That they're actually there?"

"Of course. Though we haven't been able to make contact with them in a few days, which is troubling. The reputation of that place is chilling. Lots of stories about kids being put into solitary confinement and worse. But from what I know, Benson and Trent are both physically fine."

I breathe a sigh of relief. Their situation is far from ideal, but the boys being sent to this program explains a lot. Like why their parents aren't out looking for them. And why they don't want anyone to know where they are. It also means they weren't taken by Chrissy Lambert's old boyfriend as part of some decades-long revenge plot. That I was wrong about that.

But does this mean *Jackson's* safe?

"I know a good constitutional lawyer if you need one," I finally manage to say. "Actually, it's his daughter. I know his daughter. But I'm sure he could help you. Or them. Or whatever."

Jackson smiles. "Good to know."

"It sounds like you've been doing a lot of planning out here," I tell him. "What's next?"

"Well, first off, I'm changing my name. My last name, at least."

"To what?"

"I'm not sure yet. Got any ideas?" he asks.

"Something memorable," I say. "And no puns. Or allegories."

He laughs. "You don't think Jackson the Disruptor has a good ring to it?"

"Absolutely not."

"Well, I'll keep you updated. Meanwhile, I'd like to do something positive here on this property. Find a way to help other teens who need it. Not just rich ones from Seacrest, either. Maybe we could provide shelter for kids experiencing homelessness. I don't know yet. But I also want to go to school someday. College, you know?"

By this point, the black SUV is turning into the drive, tires crunching on gravel, and I look at Jackson pleadingly. "Are you sure you can trust him? Are you absolutely sure?"

"*I'm* sure," he says. "But your relationship is your own. You should talk to him."

"He lied to me."

"So did I." Jackson looks up. Waves as Dr. Wingate steps out of the vehicle onto the driveway and into the warmth of the day. I observe him closely and with wariness, trying to knock my childhood memories loose. To see if I recognize that figure who walked into the barn and sent a chill throughout my body all those years ago.

Is it really him?

How did I not know?

"People change," Jackson says. "It's why I don't ask about monsters anymore."

"How can you know they've changed?"

"It's what they do. Not what they say." Jackson looks at his watch. "I'd better go."

I hug him tight. "I'll miss you."

"This isn't goodbye." He squeezes me close. "And that's thanks to you. You saved me, Bea. You're the reason I'm still here."

"You saved yourself," I tell him.

39

I APPROACH THE SUV WITH both caution in my heart and danger in my mind. I want to believe all that Jackson's told me about Dr. Wingate.

That people can change.

That the villain can become the hero.

He's always known my identity, I realize. Well, maybe not at the very start, but close. When I'd told him, as a child, that I'd watch my friend get beat up by his grandfather and wondered whether I had a moral obligation to tell an adult, to tell the authorities, little did I know that he'd seen the very same thing.

Because he'd been there. He'd been *here*.

So what was his moral obligation?

I walk right up to him, a wind of fury blowing at my back. "Did you know?"

"Beatrice," he says.

"Did you know what Jackson's grandfather was doing? Did you know he was killing people? Did you *help* him?"

"No," he says. "Well, yes, I figured it out eventually. I'm the one who turned him in to the FBI. But it took years for them to build a case, and I never helped him. Not once. I wanted

to stop him. Look, I can explain everything. I promise. Why don't I do that while I drive you back home?"

I square my shoulders. "No way. Let's do it here. With other people around."

"Fine."

"How did you meet Jackson's grandfather?"

"It was while I was on a leave of absence from MIT. I'd become disillusioned with my studies once I discovered how many unethical activities my professors and my *government* had willfully engaged in. Not just MKUltra or the stuff you always hear about, but other unethical experiments, like—"

"Feeding irradiated Quaker Oats to orphans?"

He nods approvingly. "Yes, that's right. You see, I'd found Jack Sr. through an online database he kept, chronicling all sorts of human rights violations and abuses of power across the United States. Operation Sea-Spray. The Tuskegee study of untreated syphilis. The Willowbrook experiment. The Tudor Monster Study. And the worst atrocity, in my mind, was something I'd never even heard of. Operation Paperclip."

"What was that?"

"Oh, just the post–World War II US government offering unconditional visas to a number of Nazi scientists and doctors and allowing them to continue their work here—often to great glory and acclaim—while never having to answer for their war crimes. It's beyond shameful."

"Why would the government want those people here?" I ask.

His face clouds with anger. "The explanation given is that it was better to import these war criminals for our own gain rather than let other countries get to them first. But that's like robbing a drug dealer and saying it's better for you to sell the drugs at profit than letting someone else do it. We don't need to get into it right now, but the next time you hear politicians use phrases like 'defending democracy' or 'nation building,' ask yourself if the accompanying actions are any different from what might be called an 'invasion' or 'ethnic cleansing,' if it were carried out by our enemies."

"Oh," I say.

"I'm sorry. I'm getting too political. I realize this."

"It's fine."

"None of it's fine, but this is what I'm passionate about. Psychiatry, psychology, the nature of human behavior, it can all be political, sure, but it doesn't have to be partisan. That's what I want the world to understand. No matter what side you're on, you can't rationalize cruelty because you see yourself as the hero. By definition, a hero isn't cruel." He shakes his head. "Look, I don't want to sugarcoat my role in this. At the time, I was young and angry and suspicious of authority and probably had some extremist tendencies of my own. It's the reason Jack's work spoke to me. It's why I contacted him about his database, and I was thrilled when he invited me out here for a series of interviews that I used in my final thesis when I finally returned to my studies. Then, years later, after finishing my residency, I came out here to write.

Jack offered me a free place to stay, although by then I saw him less as a mentor and more just lonely. He'd recently been widowed, and his only son had defied his father's hatred of the government by joining the military after 9/11."

"Defending democracy," I say.

"Now you're getting it." He smiles, pushes his hair back. "Well, two things of significance happened that summer. The first was Jack introducing me to a beautiful young woman from Cabot Cove. Her very wealthy family owned another nearby farm and she rode competitively, which is how she'd met Jack. We were pretty much opposites, but as such things tend to happen, a romance sparked between us. One that was never built to last because I soon learned that this young woman was already engaged to Jack's son. The soldier who was off at war. I felt awful and broke it off, but not before—well, I'm sure you can guess the rest."

"Jackson!" I clap a hand over my mouth. "Oh my god. You're his *father*."

"That's right. Although I didn't know that then. But Marla must have. The timing was . . . evident."

"Is *that* why Jackson's dad hates him?"

"It probably has something to do with it."

"Wait. Have you talked with her lately? Jackson's mom? Because she kind of sucks. And she *scratched* me."

"Beatrice . . ."

"Go on. I'm sorry. This is just a lot."

"I understand."

I wave my hand. "Tell me the rest. I'll be quiet. I promise."

"That summer was also the first time I got a real hint at Jack's cruelty. That's the other thing that happened. I began to understand he'd purposely pushed Marla and I together in order to punish his son. For someone so determined to expose hypocrisy and abuses of power, it seemed he was equally prone to both. I started getting suspicious about the bombings once I realized they coincided with some of the events we'd discussed. He'd taken his website down by then, but I'd documented most of it, years prior, and could make the connections. But near the end, he really just victimized people out of spite. There was no cause or agenda to his actions. He killed a horse breeder in Kentucky who badmouthed one of his stallions. A car salesman he thought had ripped him off. The randomness of it took me a while to figure out, but once I did, I went straight to the FBI and started working with them. Even then it took years, and during that time, I had to maintain the illusion that we were friends. It was very stressful."

I quickly do the math in my head. "So then you *were* here, right? At the same time I was?"

He nods. "Just that one day. Jack didn't tell me anything about children visiting. It was almost as if he'd forgotten you were here."

"He hit your *son*," I say. "And you didn't stop him."

Dr. Wingate's expression is pained. "I know. I still feel sick about that. It was all I could do not to hit him back that day. I pulled him off, made sure Jackson wasn't more seriously hurt, and told him to run. But I was working with the feds by that point—*me!*—and I had to get Jack on tape talking about the bombings. But you cared for Jax, Bea, and you got him out of there, and for that I was so, so grateful. I vowed to move to Cabot Cove after that incident. To keep an eye on my boy. And, as it turned out, to help you do the same."

My head's spinning. I can't take this all in. "How did Jackson find out? About you? About his parents?"

"We first met face-to-face at the hospital when he was inpatient a couple years ago. Then our paths crossed again when he was studying up at Broadmoor."

"He took classes at Broadmoor?"

"Not really. He was part of some advanced science program that makes use of their labs and classrooms. The equipment's better than most colleges. That's why he was up there."

"Huh."

"Anyway, I used to run a therapy group for some of the Broadmoor students. Our schedules overlapped, and I ended up driving Jackson back and forth. Selfishly, I wanted to get to know him. Leah and I couldn't have children of our own and fatherhood had become this empty hole in my life. But I had no intention of revealing to Jackson who I really was. Or who I suspected I was. But during those drives, something happened. He started opening up to me. About how cruel his parents were—they were threatening to send him away to some terrible place because he'd gotten a B on a history exam and then Marla locked up his medication because she thought it made him lazy. His suicidal thoughts were coming back, and he felt as if that's what his parents wanted. For him to suffer. Maybe even for him to die. The situation was urgent, so I told him the truth. We did a paternity test to make sure, but once it came back, we began making plans for him to leave."

"What about this farm?"

"I ended up buying it from the bank years ago. The feds had seized it—the Glanvilles certainly didn't want it—and it felt wrong to let someone else live here when so many terrible secrets remain buried on this land. I used to lease out just the barn and riding area to a nearby summer camp. But when Jackson and I started talking more, he mentioned wanting to find a place where teens he knew who were struggling with mental health issues or abuse could stay. We were already planning for him to move out here, so I offered him co-ownership of the deed to this farm."

"What would you have told *me*?" I ask. "If I'd gone on blaming myself for Jackson's disappearance?"

Dr. Wingate tilts his head. "I think you know the answer to that question."

"Oh, right." I nod, dazed. Of *course*.

It's why I'm here.

"How are you feeling?" he asks.

"Confused. Were you ever actually my psychiatrist?"

"Always. Our meeting was entirely happenstance. I

recognized you, yes, but I didn't know anything about you or even what your relationship with Jackson was. Later, admittedly, a conflict of interest arose, but I attempted to handle it in the most ethical way possible."

"How was it ethical to let me think I was arranging for Jackson to come to your therapy group?"

"Because it was your idea. A very generous one. It wasn't my place to critique your efforts to help. And it wasn't my place to tell you anything about my relationship with Jackson."

"I don't know," I say. "Even if you were just trying to honor everyone's privacy, I don't like that you kept things from me. Things you knew I was involved in."

He dips his head. "I get it. I'd feel the same way if I were you, and it wasn't fair to put you in a position where you can't be sure you can trust me. For that I apologize."

"I think I'm ready for that ride back now."

"Are you sure?"

I look into his blue eyes. They're Jackson's eyes, I realize. That same cobalt shade and stoic intensity. Why had I not seen it before? How could I have missed it? "Do you think I could come back again sometime?"

"Absolutely."

"My phone," I say, realizing it's still in Iris's car.

But Dr. Wingate holds it up like a magic trick. "I've got it right here."

×××

Once we're back on the road, heading out toward the coast, I have more questions. Too many. I can't hold back.

“The library?” I ask. “What happened there? Who burned it? And why?”

“That I don’t know,” he says.

“Come on.”

“I really don’t.”

“But someone did it to protect you.”

Dr. Wingate frowns, holding the wheel tighter. “What do you mean?”

“My friend Leisl was in there looking at old yearbooks. We were trying to find out who Chrissy Lambert’s old boyfriend was. The scholarship kid who went to MIT. But I mean, that’s you, right? You’re the boyfriend.”

“Wait, what?” He stares at me. “I read your column after you asked me to, but that wasn’t me. What on earth gave you that idea?”

“Hmm, let’s see. Well, his name starts with *A*. He went to Broadmoor. He’d be your age . . .” I count off the likenesses with my hand. “It *has* to be you. Although admittedly, for a second there, I thought you might be a serial killer. Or at least a kidnapper. Like the Pied Piper. Luring the Seacrest children into the woods as payback for their mothers and grandmothers lying about Chrissy’s death.”

His eyes bulge. “You actually thought I did that?”

“Briefly! Just briefly.”

“You briefly thought I *killed children*?”

“I have a morbid imagination,” I say.

“Beatrice, I’m aware of this fact, but still . . .”

I sit up in my seat, lift my chin. “Yeah, well, I never

imagined that you would've gotten together with *Marla Glanville*, of all people. So life's full of surprises."

"Touché."

I crack a smile.

"Well, I'm not a serial killer and I'm also not Chrissy's ex-boyfriend. My name does start with *A*, true, but I wasn't on scholarship, and also, I didn't know Chrissy. Not well at least, although I remember when she died. It was very sad."

I rub my temple. Now I'm more confused than ever. "Do you know who it might've been? He would've graduated in the mid-eighties sometime."

"I was eighty-seven. But I don't remember any other students going to MIT. Math isn't what Broadmoor is known for. Or it wasn't at the time."

"Well, maybe he didn't end up going. He attended an admitted student event, though."

"Ah." Dr. Wingate nods slowly. "Then I think I might know who you're talking about. Let me do some reaching out. If I recall, he was pretty messed up after what happened, and I've lost track of what he's doing or where he lives. His younger brother, however, is a member of local law enforcement and could certainly get the info to him. I'm sure he'd be grateful to have closure over that girl's death."

"But he left her!" I cry. "And he took money to do it. He's not innocent in this."

Dr. Wingate sighs. "You don't know that that's true. You just know what Chrissy's father told her, and it sounds like he didn't always tell the truth."

I fold my arms and sulk a little. I don't like that answer or being asked to empathize with a guy who might've abandoned his girlfriend and let her believe she wasn't worth fighting for.

We sit in silence after that, moving through the trees, the towns. For some reason, I keep tapping my knee in a rhythmic fashion.

Something's not right. I'm missing something.

Again.

"Tenace," I say abruptly as we cross the Cove County line.

"What's that now?" Dr. Wingate looks over at me.

"The game. I know you know what I'm talking about. Did you play? While you were at Broadmoor? You must have."

Now a smile twists his lips. "If I did, I couldn't tell you."

"I'll take that as a yes." I grip the front of my seat belt. "Okay, but here's what I don't get. Who runs the game? Who sets up the red markers and clues and orchestrates this whole thing? Because none of it's random, is it? These are real mysteries students are being asked to solve. But mysteries that maybe people don't even know exist."

"What're you talking about?"

"Like Chrissy Lambert," I say. "Or the HOA thing. Or even the truth about Jackson."

"Are those really part of the game?" he asks.

"Aren't they?"

"What if I were to tell you," he begins, "that the game's run by previous winners or players who came close to winning? And that maybe the reason they did well in the first place is that they're people who have their own mysteries that need to be put out into the world. And that maybe it's also possible that, whether or not these mysteries ever get solved, just having a collective sense of energy put into understanding them can be restorative."

"I don't get it," I say.

"You don't have to. But know this. That fire in the library—it means something."

"What if it's just a coincidence?" I ask.

"Is that really what you think?"

"Hold on." I turn to stare at him. "You *won*, didn't you? That's what you're telling me. You won the game. And so did Chrissy Lambert's boyfriend. Whoever he is. He must've also won. Right? Or came close?"

Dr. Wingate doesn't answer.

Ten minutes later, we pull up in front of my house. It's late afternoon. My father's car is gone and the yard's covered in leaves. Our maple's branches are finally bare.

"Who's going to be my doctor now?" I ask Dr. Wingate. "Is it you?"

"If you want me to be," he says.

"I need to think about it."

"Of course."

"Thanks for the ride," I say.

"It's the least I could do." He glances out at the street around him. "And Bea?"

HOME ABOUT NEWS ARCHIVE

TRUEMAINE.COM

Home Page for the State of Maine . . . and Murder . . .

"Stepping into the Spectacle"

This will just be a quick update, as I'm sure most of you are aware of what's been going on in Cabot Cove over the last week. If not, check out our special report: "Tragedy of the Commons: A Story of Greed, Power, and Parental Cruelty in a Small Town HOA" written by staff writer and TrueMaine cofounder Aaron Kanofsky. It details the ethical questions brought up by the revelation that a group of wealthy Cabot Cove parents conspired to surveil their own children and have the rebellious ones abducted and sent to a "troubled teen" program in Utah known for its "tough love" approach and history of lawsuits. Not only did these parents file fraudulent missing person reports in order to make their children feel abandoned, but it appears that one family—the Mulvaneys—has financial ties to the company that runs the Utah program and others like it.

If you're still not caught up, you can also read the *Central Cove Gazette*'s very lengthy article, "Seacrest Homeowners Association Accused of Child Abuse, Kidnapping, Fraud, and Bribery," by Sage Morello, which describes the brave actions of two teens who escaped their own abusive homes and potential abductions and set out to save their friends. With the help of Sheriff's Deputy Charles Williams, a dogged detective who's been able to document the group's history of fraud and bribery over a span of more than fifteen years, the DA's office expects grand jury indictments to be handed down soon, with possible federal charges also forthcoming. Finally, I'll be posting my own interview with Deputy Williams in the very near future to discuss the unlikely connection among these HOA members, the deputy's older brother, Dr. Adam Williams, and Chrissy Lambert's tragic death more than thirty years ago.

And with that, let me know in the comments if there's a new cold case you think I should be focusing on. Also, please note that my name has changed. Previously I'd written under a pseudonym mostly because of general shyness and a desire to hide behind the curtain of anonymity. But I don't want to hide anymore, and I can't detach myself from the stories I write about. Who I am fundamentally informs how I see the world and why I care so deeply about loss and death. I don't want to lose sight of that, and I also want to be accountable for what I create.

So hello, TrueMaine readers. I'm Beatrice Fletcher, a high school student currently attending Cabot Cove High. It's good to finally meet you.

Yours truly,

—Bea

Sign up for our newsletter!

Epilogue

It's freezing when I climb the ladder. I'm wearing a dress and leggings and boots, but it's not enough. Not even close. Barely November and it already feels like winter's overtaken us.

Once inside the treehouse, I resume my search. I'd thought I'd been thorough the last time I was here, but apparently not. Now that I have more clear direction, I dig around in the milk crate where the cans of food and water sit and finally, through the grated holes in the bottom of the crate, I spot it. A tiny door's been cut into the floorboard.

Shoving the crate aside, I use a screwdriver to lift the wooden cutout only to reveal a small space under the floorboards. I reach in and find what I'm looking for.

Two envelopes.

The first has my name written on the front. I drop to the floor beneath the narrow window for light and open it.

Dear Bea,

By the time you read this, I'll be gone, having left to start a new life—my life—on my own terms. I'm sorry I couldn't tell you earlier, although I hope you'll understand why it was necessary to do this the way that I did. My other hope is that you find this letter quickly and can be assured that I'm safe and alive and have no intention of harming myself or allowing myself to be harmed ever again.

I know there's a chance you'll feel betrayed, by me or by Dr. Wingate or the fact that we knew each other before you tried so valiantly to connect us. But in a way, you did connect us—both years ago on my grandfather's farm and then again, in eighth grade, when you helped keep me alive, despite all my impulses to the contrary.

For that and for everything, I will always be grateful. To some degree, I know that your loyalty to me comes from the promise I made in second grade to never let you feel alone or like you didn't have someone who would be there for you. But I also know that I haven't been able to fulfill this promise in recent years. I've tried and I've wanted to, but depression can be cruel that way. It smothers things like desire and love and intention. It twists kindness into guilt and duty into shame, and I know now that I have to take care of myself before I can be the friend you deserve.

This is all just a long way of explaining why I've chosen to leave the way I have. Not just to keep my parents from finding out where I've gone before I want them to, but to offer you what I hope can be a gift—a *connection to a group of like-minded friends who love mystery and wonder just as much as you do.*

Until then,

J, your most uncouth swain

XXX

I press the letter to my chest after reading, closing my eyes and allowing my emotions to wash over me. A lot is confusion and sorrow, but what I feel most deeply is gratitude. Not just for Jackson's safety and the fact he's found a sense of family and belonging, but that he's been in my life at all. For all my lamenting over my inability to forge deep relationships and genuine intimacy, haven't I always known, deep down, that this wasn't true? That, for both Jax and I, our sense of guardedness and stubborn reluctance has been born more from self-preservation than character flaw?

That *this*, what he and I have, is unbreakable?

It takes me a while, but when I'm ready, I neatly fold his letter and slide it back into its envelope. Then I crawl out of the treehouse, emerging into daylight by skipping the last few rungs and jumping to the ground with a dramatic thud. Leisl turns around first, followed by Carlos and Leif. They're all smiling at me. Grinning, really.

"You *knew*?" I ask. "All of you?"

"Just Carlos," Leif says. "But he told us about it this morning on our way to meet you. Crazy, huh?"

Leisl sighs dramatically. "Carlos is good with secrets. Too good. It's absolutely his worst quality."

"How'd you meet him?" I ask Carlos.

"Science seminar. I'm not in the advanced program that he was, but I got to sit in on some of the lectures. We got to talking."

"So Jax knew about tenace?"

"Not a lot, I don't think. But enough to ask questions. Enough to get me to agree to do my part that night in the woods, with the promise that you'd help us in return. I didn't know any of the context, though, other than that he wanted us to be kind to you and play along with the idea that you'd been chased. I really thought it was part of the game. That maybe you were, too."

I shake my head, amazed.

"You were also supposed to find that letter a lot earlier," he says. "When we met that day at the coffee shop, I was trying to subtly find a way to get you out here . . ."

"You were?"

"Emphasis on the word *trying*."

"Thanks for that." I smile and know better than to say that reason we didn't meet up again after that was because of Leisl's warning.

"I'm just sorry you had to suffer for so long," Carlos says.

"I think everything worked out the way it was supposed to. Well, except for this. I was probably meant to find this earlier, as well, and give it to you." Now I hold up the second envelope I'd pulled from the floorboard hiding spot.

The red one.

For a moment, they're all silent, as if considering what to say or not say or what any of it might mean.

Leif speaks first. "Well, no wonder we haven't advanced for the past two weeks! Did *you* know that was there?"

Carlos shakes his head.

"You really expect me to believe that?" Leif counters.

"Maybe you can't," Carlos replies.

Leisl bites her lip. "This feels wrong somehow. That clue means we've gone out of order. What if not finding it when we were meant to is connected to the fire? Maybe someone thinks we already have it, and they assume we know something we don't. Or . . ."

"Or what?" her brother asks.

"Or maybe the fire was a way for the game to redirect our attention to where we're supposed to be looking. Like a built-in correction."

"Oh please. Stop with that crazy stuff, already." Leif shoots an exasperated look at Carlos and me. "Lately she's been buying into this whole metaphysical 'the game is also a player' theory. On account of the game nearly killing her. Go figure. It's totally messed with her head."

"*I'm* not the crazy one," Leisl mutters.

"Enough," her brother snaps. "Anyway, my money's on that creepy cop burning down the library. The one who told Bea that he knows who we are."

"I don't think that's right," I say.

"That cop *does* know who we are," Leisl insists. "You

just don't remember. He was there last year when we were searching for . . . you know."

A faint memory flickers through my mind. "You mean Eden, right?"

Leisl nods.

I snap my fingers. "That's where I know him from! It's where I know you from, too. We were all part of the same search party. The one where we were denied access to that home on Lake Paloma."

Carlos's shoulders slump at the mention of Eden, and Leisl reaches to take his hand.

"Maybe that could be right," she tells me.

Maybe?

Leif waves impatiently at the envelope I'm still holding. "Enough stalling. Open it already. Let's do this."

"You want *me* to open it?"

"Of course," he says. "You're a part of this now, aren't you?"

Both Leisl and Carlos murmur in agreement, urging me on, and even though this is what Jax, ever the insistent shepherd, wanted for me, I can't help but hesitate, unsure of how to feel about these three and what accepting their invitation into gameplay might actually mean. Is it being offered in honest, good faith? And if so, is it *me* they truly want by their side? Or am I stepping into the role of a dead girl?

A girl I tried to find but never knew.

I can't answer these questions just like I can't see into their hearts and minds and know their truths. But I can't do that with anyone, a reality that's haunted me for years and held me back from making and doing and being to the full.

Then again, there's only one choice, opening the envelope, that will take me where I can't bear not to go—down a spiraling rabbit hole of mystery.

And intrigue.

And wonder.

So in another way, there's really no choice for me at all.

TO BE CONTINUED . . .

Acknowledgments

In challenging times, this book has been a joy to work on. Not only was I able to revisit a world I'd grown up watching, but it was also a world that inspired me to become a writer. It showed me women could be brilliant, successful, clever, and kind, and that it was far more thrilling to watch a woman solve a murder than be a victim of one.

I am so thankful to everyone who has collaborated and helped me through this process. Working with people equally enthusiastic about spending time in present-day Cabot Cove has meant everything. Many, many thanks to Michael Bourret for his endless support and guidance, and to my wonderful editor, Jenne Abramowitz, whose creativity, insight, and enthusiasm have been invaluable. Thank you to Keirsten Geise, Katt Phatt, Rachel Feld, Shannon Pender, Mary Kate Garmire, and everyone at Scholastic who has worked so hard to put this book into the world. Thank you also to Michael Moccio for his wit and encouragement, as well as Susan Weber, and the entire team at NBCUniversal. Finally, thank you to my family. Will, Sid, Tessa, and Severin, you are my everything.

About the Author

Stephanie Kuehn is a clinical psychologist and an award-winning author of six novels for teens, including *Charm & Strange*, which won the ALA's 2014 William C. Morris Award for best debut young adult novel. *Booklist* has praised her work as "Intelligent, compulsively readable literary fiction with a dark twist." As a lifelong *Murder, She Wrote* fan, Stephanie recently introduced the series to her own teenagers, who now share her love of mystery and all things Cabot Cove.